JOHN FRUM
THE RELUCTANT MESSIAH

ROBERT BUCKLEY

To my pack, who upon hearing of this crazy idea went out and had John Frum T-shirts printed up.
Mary, Kyle and Jessi, you are my world.

PREFACE

"For verily I say unto you, That whosoever shall say unto this moutain, Be thou removed, and be thou cast into the sea, and shall not doubt in his heart, but shall believe that those things which he saith shall come to pass, he shall have whatsoever he saith." Mark 11:23, King James Bible

It was going to happen, it had to. This was her mountain and it was about to be cast into the sea.

Firmly planting her feet beside the overturned mini-van and with all the strength her 128 lb. frame could muster, she screamed in defiance of her odds and lifted the crumpled, metal monster that was ruthlessly pinning her child to the ground.

At one time or another we've all been captured by a news story of the impossible suddenly becoming possible. There is no rational explanation, and yet as humans we feel compelled to find an explanation for the unexplainable. The answer, if there is one, is complicated but what I can tell you, is that the immutable Law of Believing is always at it's core. You know, believing is receiving? That simple, overused phrase that shows up on everything from an inspirational office poster to the side of a secret santa coffee mug. The tendency is to cynically discount such things, but the funny thing is, believing is like gravity. It doesn't require your belief in it for it to work. It just works, every time.

I've long been intrigued by that verse. As I see it, there are three possibilities of it's meaning. It's either a bold face lie or to be kind, an exageration or merely a metaphor to serve as inspiration to all who persevere in the face of insurmountable odds. Or lastly, and most interestingly, a simple truth, hidden in plain sight to be taken literally on it's face, that holds the keys to unfathomnable abilities beyond our wildest imagination. If it is that simple, then it begs the question, why don't we see this in evidence more often? The answer is in the verse's only caveat- "and shall not doubt in his heart."

Doubt. The biggest obstacle to the occurence of the super natural is the elimination of doubt. After all, doubt is believing in reverse, a contradiction, working contrary to the goal. To obscure all doubt in your heart, the core of your being, is seemingly impossible. One would have to have been raised in a world without limitations, without circumstances brought on by western culture and modern civilization. As far as I know, only one person in recorded history has ever managed to pull that off- and He was born with it.

So I asked myself a question. What if someone had the ability to turn doubt off, like a light switch, whenever he or she needed to? What would that person be capable of, what would be possible, what remarkable things would we, and the world for that matter, see? Meet John Frum.

CHAPTER 1

THE QUIZ

I t should have come as no surprise to John that traffic on Hamilton Street would be so unrelenting. But here he was, sitting on a borrowed ten-speed waiting for that never-to-come break in traffic. He was close enough to see the outline of Professor Wharton, pacing as he policed his class through the University's second-story windows. But he might as well have been a million miles away. It was test day and he was late...again.

"Come on, come on, come on!" he said in exasperation. Glancing at his watch, the second hand taunted him with each faint tick, tick, tick, tick...

With his gaze fixed upon its face, he lowered his head ever so slightly and exhaled in one long, single, solitary breath. The second hand slowed and then with one final tick...

Stopped.

In complete silence, he entered traffic and began weaving his way miraculously through. It was as if he had somehow mapped out the space between his own molecules and those of the speeding cars around him, and skillfully navigated his way through it, matter through matter. It was the stuff of a Hollywood movie scene filmed in slow motion. An overhead drones-eye view of blurred cars whizzing in opposite directions and the laser-focused clarity of John pedaling forward unscathed. But it wasn't. It was real.

Suddenly popping out the other side, the otherworldly silence was replaced by the chaotic sounds of heavy traffic slamming back in as he sped towards the brick-framed stairway. Dismounting with the skill of a rodeo performer, John leaped from his bike. It continued forward, banging into the bike rack and in one last mini miracle, managed to remain perfectly upright in its slot.

Peering down from the lecture hall, Professor Wharton had witnessed the entire event. His expression, however, was curiously blasé, almost annoyed. Surely not what one would expect from someone who had just witnessed an event that was nothing short of supernatural.

John took the stairs two at a time. Carefully opening the door and hoping to go unnoticed, he attempted to quietly melt into his seat.

"Ahhh! Mr. Ferrum. Consistency! A most admirable trait was it not for the fact that yours is being consistently late. You have exactly..." Professor Wharton looked at his watch. "Two and a half minutes to complete your quiz." He smiled and motioned to the quiz on John's desk. "Mr. Ferrum?"

John raised a finger, as to ward him off, his eyes in half-shut concentration. He began slowly at first and then with an ever-increasing cadence, checked off each multiple-choice answer. Professor Wharton rolled his eyes, turned, and retreated to his podium.

One quick glance at John, he sighed and called out, "Time ladies and gentlemen."

The once quiet room erupted in the sound of scuffing chairs and chatter as the students filed towards the professor's desk. Each handed in the completed quiz and returned to their seats. John was last.

Professor Wharton leaned in and quietly asked, "I watched you nearly kill yourself- for this?" motioning towards the quiz.

"I knew I'd be ok," John said.

"How? How'd you know?" The professor tried to pin him down.

John shrugged. "I just...knew."

After a momentary stare between them, Wharton adjusted his glasses and turned his attention to the class.

"Alright, settle please." Rolling up his sleeves, he ran his hand through his thick, white hair that was in perpetual need of a trim and began his lecture. "Picking up from where we left off yesterday."

He headed to the overhead projector, flipped on the light, and adjusted the focus. Old black and white photos of the Cargo Cult sitting, waiting on a makeshift dirt airstrip came into view.

"So, we were discussing the Cargo Cult mentality as it pertains to business. Just as primitive societies mistakenly mimic the actions of a civilized society in expectation and hope of reaping its benefits- i.e., its cargo- so do modern businesses mistakenly expect similar benefits even when entire marketing strategies are built on assumed and often, flawed premises."

The professor sucked in a huge gulp of air in preparation for his next run-on sentence.

"If you build entire hypotheses on assumption or unproven fact-"

"Like Darwinism," John muttered under his breath.

9

Professor Wharton abruptly stopped and turned. "Care to add Mr. Ferrum?" he said. John motioned no. "I insist, please!" the professor said, mockingly.

Seated next to John was his roommate, Ethan. Ethan, who came from money and suffered from black envy while simultaneously *being* black, shifted uncomfortably in his seat while whispering through his clenched, brilliantly white teeth. "Oh, dear God in heaven! Don't. No. Don't! Just don't!"

"Like Darwinism," John responded boldly. "Cargo Cult science. All the trappings of real science but a lack of basis in honest experimentation."

Collective moans could be heard from the class that knew all too well how this would play out. Professor Wharton had a reputation for derailing many a lecture when given the opportunity to espouse Darwinism at every possible chance he had. Those who were the least bit savvy knew to avoid the subject at all cost.

"Theory presented as fact, when in reality, each fact is predicated on what could easily be, and most likely IS....a flawed premise. Mimicking science."

"Sort of like the way you took your quiz?" queried the professor. John looked puzzled.

"Your quiz." Professor Wharton motioned towards the stack on his desk. "You know, you 'mimicked' your more advanced, civilized, fellow students by checking off your answers and are now expecting to reap the same results of those who actually studied." The class, feeling John was about to be owned, let out a series of oohs and stifled chuckles.

"I believe I did, uh...." John stammered.

"Let's test your theory. Let's check the answers, shall we?" replied the professor.

Professor Wharton placed John's answer sheet on the overhead projector's table and married it with the pre-punched holes of the answer grid. Almost every answer was wrong. John's look of confusion and disbelief was quickly wiped away by the sudden ringing of the class bell.

"Have a good weekend everyone" the professor bellowed.

Professor Wharton turned, and stared out the large windows, his hands clasped behind his back. The boisterous class began gathering their things and shuffled out of the room and into the crowded hallway. The sudden contrasting silence as the heavy wooden door shut behind the last student assured him he was now alone. The professor ambled over to the overhead and stood staring, looking down with eyes of both curiosity and dread at the answer grid. With one last, reassuring glance towards the door, he nonchalantly placed a finger on the bottom of the grid. Hesitating, he pushed the answer grid up slowly so that now, both top edges were correctly aligned. His eyes narrowed as he peered at the bright image on the screen. Every single answer was right. Without so much as an ounce of astonishment, only the subtle raising of an eyebrow, the professor sighed and flipped the projector's light switch to black.

CHAPTER 2

THE RED WITCH

The Red Witch. It had been the place to go since it opened in 1978 but it was tired. As far as anyone could recall, the only renovation involved the once yearly removal of the makeshift 'B' that pledging freshman would place over the 'W' of the outdoor sign on the building's roof. The sticky floors and ever-present smell of stale beer only added to the ambiance, but one thing was for sure- it had the ladies. The seriously hot ladies and well, let's face it, then and now, nothing else really mattered. A pyramid of spent beer bottles dominated most of the table's square footage as Ethan returned with yet another round.

Everyone was pleasantly buzzed and quickly stripped him of his generous booty.

"Locusts!" Ethan yelled. He popped the top on the remaining bottle, took a swig while turning to John.

"Darwin. Really? Darwin? You thought that would be a good idea?"

John finished his first sip and looked at Ethan. "Look, I can't seem to get rid of this guy. I know he's friends with my Uncle and all. But every semester since I started here, I end up with him in at least one class. And every class-"

"He never shuts up about Darwin!" a voice from another table shouted.

"Thank You!" John shouted back, raising his beer in a bottle salute.

"So, not a fan of Darwinism, eh? But dude, that was EPIC!" said Jay as he pulled up a seat.

"I don't know what I believe but it sure isn't Darwinism," responded John. "I'm supposed to believe that this kind of perfection started out as pond scum?" He lifted his shirt and pointed to his well-defined six-pack.

"Put it away Ferrum!" shouted Max from across the room. There was Max. John's hefty, unkempt, less than cerebral type buddy busy chatting up the local talent while smoking a ridiculously large neon purple vape pipe. John tried in vain to avoid Max's gaze.

"Ferrum!" Max bellowed. Caught, John reluctantly turned.

"Max! or should I say...Zamphir, master of the Pan flute?" The clever reference was lost on Max whose confused-looking face was now engulfed in a cloud of swirling, white vapor.

"Your...whatever that thing is," John said, pointing to his purple contraption.

"You're not the only one with a six-pack, Ferrum. Some of us just choose to carry it on the side." With that, Max pulled up his worn, ill-fitting Jethro Tull T-shirt revealing his blindingly white, corn-fed torso. At the same time, a group of hot girls walked by.

"Sorry ladies, he's taken," noted Jay.

"No, no, no, I'm not! " said Max. The girls giggled and scampered away towards the ladies' room. He turned to Jay and with all the seriousness he could muster said, "Hey, big bones run in the family."

Without missing a beat Jay shot back with a full dose of reality. "From the looks of things Max?" shaking his head, "nobody runs in your family."

Unfazed Max seated himself at the table and proceeded to convene a meeting. "Ok. I figured out how we're gonna make spring break money." Max turned to John. "By the way Ferrum, did I mention how much fun it was to spank your sorry ass in Battlefield last night?"

"Pffft, I've developed some mad piloting skills and you know it- If it wasn't for me, you'd still be sucking your thumb wandering around the Caspian Border looking for a way out," John said.

Unfazed, Max continued. "Alright, so here's"-

"Wait, wait, wait!" interrupted Ethan.

"What's your problem, Dufus?" an annoyed Max asked.

Ethan slammed down an empty bottle on the table. "*THAT*, my friend is the problem. Whose turn to buy?"

Silence. Ethan's eyes darted from face to face. More silence. "Anybody. John? Jay? Max?" Even more silence.

"Ok then," said Ethan. He leaned forward and as if speaking into an air microphone and spoke in hushed tones, "Uhhh, Alex I'll take famous movie quotes for four hundred?"

Then in his best booming game show announcer's voice proclaimed, "LADIES AND GENTLEMEN, THE LIGHTNING ROUND!!"

And so it began, as it always did when the group found themselves at an impasse. A cross between musical chairs and Jeopardy, this dispute-settling game required one person to quote a famous movie line and the next to name the character, who said it, and the movie's title. Speed was of the essence and it continued in rapid-fire succession until somebody fumbled and was unable to come up with the answer in time.

Reluctantly at first John threw out the first ball. " That wasn't flying, that was falling with style."

Seated to John's right Ethan quickly answered, "Woody- *Toy Story*. I'm not bad, I'm just drawn that way."

They looked to a nerdy underclassman to Ethan's right. "I'm the DD, remember?" Everyone nodded in a chorus of "oh, yeah."

Jay jumped in with, "*Jessica Rabbit Who Framed Roger Rabbit?*" He took a quick sip and sang "The cold never bothered me anyway."

Max removed his vape pipe long enough to answer, "Easy! Elsa-*Frozen*. Roads? Who needs roads? Where we're goin', we don't need.... roads."

By this time, their impromptu game had begun to draw more than a few onlookers, crowding the only pathway to the ladies' room. At one point, Max's enthusiastic hand gestures inadvertently sent a passing waitress into a corner, almost toppling her and her drink-laden tray. The room immediately fell silent. All eyes were on this crucially good-looking server. She smiled at Jay.

"Nobody puts Baby in the corner," she said. Without missing a beat, a voice from two tables away shouted, "*Dirty Dancing*!" and the round continued.

"Doc Emmitt Brown," John said. "*Back to the Future*," and then added, "You smell like beef and cheese."

"Ah, man one of my favs," Ethan said. "Buddy in *Elf*. We're not hosting an intergalactic kegger down here!"

Jay, distracted by the same cornered hot waitress who continued to smile at him from behind the bar, blanked out. Just flat out blanked out. And with that ladies and gentlemen, we had a winner. Or more accurately, a loser.

"Shit," Jay fumed. The table erupted in laughter as Jay got up and headed to the bar. Over his shoulder and above the din he shouted, "Zed. *Men in Black!*"

Ethan mouthed 'thank you' to the waitress who winked back. Undaunted, Max picked right up where he left off. "Alright. Here's what we do." He proceeded to place a cheap, *Hello Kitty* pink tablet on the table.

"We sell knock-off iPads to elementary school children?" mocked Ethan.

"Thirty-nine bucks because it doesn't have an apple on it. It's just as good preppy, but no," Max scowled. "Check it out." A video of ultimate fails played evoking both laughter and groans as each painful mishap was played out on the screen.

"Ok, so?" asked Jay.

"Two words gentleman," he said, pausing to build the suspense. "Viral. Video." Max emphasized each word with double peace signs and scanned the table for reactions. "Well?" he said. Stone faces. No one was buying.

"Ya kinda got a Dick Nixon vibe goin' on there for a moment", Jay threw his arms up imitating the resigned president's now-infamous farewell photo.

"Pass me a....." John was pointing towards the newly arrived cold ones. "Yeah."

"Ughhh!!" Max's frustration began to show. "Look, we come up with a killer idea, something that's never been done before. Film it, upload it to YouTube! It goes viral, we sit back and collect the ad revenue...Simple!"

"What's your idea?" asked Ethan.

"I was kinda counting on you guys for that," Max mumbled, resulting in an uproar of collective groans and laughter. Suddenly drunks-in-training ideas were bandied about and subsequently met with choruses of "Lame! No! Oh No!" and "Oh Hell No!"

"We could always just drop some shit out of an airplane over the Cargo Cult and see them freak out, that'd be funny," Ethan suggested. Silence. Most of the group wore puzzled looks on their glazed faces.

"That is such a bad idea," John said.

"What's a Cargo Cult?" asked Max.

Ethan shook his head in disbelief. "Geez! Really? Have you attended *any* of Wharton's lectures...I mean...awake...sober? alright, so-" John interrupted, "If I may." Ethan mocked him. "If I may!"

"Let's see if I can get through this," John said. "Ok, Cliff Notes version-" He took another pull on his beer and let out a short, snappy burp. "Towards the end of WWII-" turning to Max, "the real one, not the Xbox version- Allied forces needed bases in the South Pacific to get closer to Japan."

"So, they could kick some gook ass!" Max blurted out loudly. Just then an Asian classmate walked by. The table went dead silent in disbelief. Jay asked, "Is it even possible to actually *die* of embarrassment?"

John shook his head while closing his eyes. "Wrong war. Jap ass actually." Just then John's lacrosse teammate, Gunwoo Yoojin, walked by. "Sorry dude!" John apologized.

Gunwoo laughed, "How many times do I have to tell you, I'm Korean!" and flashed him two fingers.

"So... They began to set up bases on these little-known islands, airlifting all this equipment, just dropping it in the jungle. So here we have all these natives who've never so much as even seen a white guy suddenly surrounded by all this alien hardware. They think their long gone, ancient ancestors delivered all this stuff, and they quickly grow to like it."

Jay seemed puzzled by that. "So then how would dropping stuff on them freak them out? I mean they already know about radios and TVs and stuff, right?"

"Ahhh!" John answered. "Just as quickly as it arrived, it left. The war ended, the allies packed up and left, taking their toys with them. Ever since that day, these tribes have tried to recreate the same situation thinking this would cause them to return. Hence the term, 'Cargo Cult Mentality' that Wharton was talking about? Ya' with me? They built a dirt airstrip, made a tower, planes, headphones, runway lights just like the Americans had - all out of bamboo and vines hoping that the gods would see it from above, be fooled, and come back. So, check it. They are there, today, as we speak," John pausing for effect and long enough to have a swig, "waiting for their Messiah to reappear."

"Guess what his name is?" asked Ethan. All eyes turned to Ethan who was smiling with delight. "John Frum."

"Ferrum?" Jay said.

"Funny. Frum." John corrected, "Fruuuum!"

"From where?" Max laughed at his own clever catch.

"Funny you should ask because many believe that's *exactly* how their messiah got his name. One of the GI's supposedly introduced himself to the chief saying, 'Hi I'm John from America and voile', it stuck. John From. The fact of the matter is.. he was probably black."

"Solid!" Ethan proudly exclaimed. "Now dat's what I'm talkin' about!"

"Solid?" Jay's face screwed up. Ethan rose to his own defense. "Yeah, ya' know, kinda Mod Squad- like us." Everyone quickly picked up their beers to stifle their laughter.

"That's stupid. They've been waitin' for over seventy-five years for their guy to come back?" Max asked. "Morons."

"Christians have been waiting for their guy to return for over two thousand sooo... jes sayin'," John added.

Ethan suddenly stood, his beer raised above his head and in his best black Baptist minister's voice proclaimed, "Ya gotta have faitha, my brothas and sistas, Faitha!! Cause if lovin' the lawd is wronga...." After a long, exaggerated gasp of air everyone joined him in unison.

"I don't wanna be righta! Amen!! Thank ya' Jesus!"

Jay felt a compulsion to add, "Arsenio Hall, *Coming to America!*"

"So, we film their reaction after we drop a bunch a' trinkets and crap out of an airplane," Ethan mused. "Which, of course, is pretty much impossible for us to pull off, come to think of it."

"No! No! No! This is good!" Max said. "This could work!" He turned to Jay. "Doesn't your dad still use that Boeing 314 Clipper; you know the flying boat to move his stuff around?"

"How do you remember all that?" Jay asked.

"And what about that lunatic pilot that worked for him?" Max continued.

"The crazy-ass, Keith Richards lookin' old Brit that used to buy us cigarettes and beer?" Ethan asked while pointing his beer at him.

"When we were twelve?!" Max added laughing.

John looked at them, not amused. "Aiden," he said.

"Aiden! That's right. Kinda scary," Max said. "I mean, the guy looks like a burnt-out building."

Everyone burst out in laughter. Even John had to smile at that one because as descriptions go, it was pretty accurate. Aiden had led a 'colorful' life to put it mildly and the evidence of that was written all over his face- even on a good day. John had spent a great deal of his childhood in Aiden's company and considered him a favorite 'uncle,' so it was hard to go along with all the poking fun at him. But he did have to admit, that *was* funny.

"Man, my dad would kill me," contemplated Jay.

"He's gonna kill you anyway when he finds out how you're wasting his money here at school." quipped Ethan.

Suddenly the band ripped into its first set. The music was deafening, killing any chance of continuing the conversation. With bass bins in the speaker array the size of small apartments, it was no surprise when everything began to magically move across the worn laminate table top. The crowd began to head towards the dance floor and breathable air was now becoming a scarce commodity. John threw back what was left in his rocks glass, winced, and began to get up. Jay looked at him with a rather puzzled look.

"Just goin' for some air," John said.

Jay, yelling over the music, "What?"

"AIR!" John yelled while pantomiming a deep breath. "Besides, the drink price just went up," nodding towards the band.

"Told you not to mix dark with clear."

"What?"

Jay motioned to never mind. John turned and made his way through the steamy, gyrating partiers that had now crowded onto the tiny dance floor. He headed towards the front door and as usual, admiring glances were cast his way by a few of the prowling, Cosmo-sipping ladies as he attempted to slip by. Jay and Max followed him out, stopping to address one of the female admirers.

"Bitch, do not be eyeballin' my man!" Jay snapped. Her mouth dropped open, taken aback at what she just heard but then turned to laughter as Jay snapped his fingers in her face, turned and with hips in motion, sashayed out the front door.

Once outside, John moved away from the noisy front door and leaned against a convenient FedEx drop-off box. Instinctively, he pulled his phone from his front pocket to check it but was quickly distracted by a sound coming from the darkened alley in front of him. Squinting to clear both his vision and his brain, he made out the silhouette of a large man pinning a much smaller woman against the wall. It became clear to him that the sounds he was hearing were not those of inebriated partiers, rather that of someone in distress- a woman that wanted no part of what was about to go down.

"Hey!" yelled John instinctively. The man stopped and turned to look at John and in so doing revealed a bit more of himself in the shadowy light. He was all of 6'7", almost as broad with large garish features. It was just enough of a distraction that the woman was able to break away from him and run out the other side of the alley. He started to walk towards John, the reason for his lost prey, and he. was. pissed.

"Oh, shit," breathed John. He could have run, but the same alcohol-fuel bravado that caused him to call out in the first place still had hold of him. Stand your ground, he thought. By the time reason had a chance to seep its way into his marinated brain, it was too late. This monster of a man was upon him, his face gnarled into a rabid, animal-like countenance. John assumed a fighting stance and grimaced in the expectation of the first pounding blow. But it never came. Suddenly, not two feet from him, the beast's face had a look of sheer terror. One last look of astonishment towards John and without warning, he was violently whisked into some sort of invisible vortex. It seemed to stretch his body backward like a Saturday morning cartoon of being sucked into a giant vacuum cleaner. The snapback of the closing of this portal sent a shock wave so great that it lifted John and threw him to the ground, flat on his back. Max and Jay exited the noisy bar just in time to witness John falling backward to the ground.

"Did you see that!? Tell me you saw that!!" John exclaimed.

"Yeah!" Max said. "Looked really stupid."

"No! no! no! I mean..."

Jay interrupted. "What did I tell you!? Don't mix dark with clear! Bad shit happens when you do that. C'mon, let's go back inside before you *really* hurt yourself."

"Wait, wait!" John protested. "There was this huge guy and..."

Jay and Max hauled a protesting John back into the bar where John continued his attempt at explaining what had just happened, but the music was so deafening all they saw was a fully animated, wide-eyed, hand flailing John mouthing the words and half acting out this bizarre event. Halfway back to the table they were met by Ethan.

"C'mon, we're movin' this party to Abby's apartment," Ethan said. "We lost our table. What's with him? Looks like he just saw a ghost."

"Oh, man! Do you know how hard it is to get that table? *That* table? The one that's right by the only path to the ladies' room?" Max whined.

"What!? You guys took off and they bum-rushed me... and there were a lot of them... and they can smell fear," replied Ethan sheepishly.

A look over his shoulder revealed their much-coveted table now overrun with hot club chicks and male worker bees buzzing around the newly formed hive.

CHAPTER 3

ABBY'S APARTMENT

"*L*A woman! LA woman!*"*

L With the Doors' Jim Morrison wailing away through speakers that were permanently mounted to the pillars of her front porch, Abby's duplex apartment was easy enough to spot. The lights, the music, the vehicle-littered lawn - all a dead giveaway. No one had ever really met Abby, at least not that they knew of, and everyone always assumed that her next-door neighbors were either deaf or dead. But her monthly parties were the stuff of legend and tonight was no exception. They made their way in, grabbed another red cup of God-only-knows, and proceeded to scope the place out. Ethan, the good friend he was, swooped in to claim a rare seat on the worn, threadbare velvet sectional for a dazed and confused John. Still trying to sort out what had just happened, John stared straight ahead, fighting to stay awake through his drunk goggles while pinned between Max and Jay.

"Dude, you're seriously flipped out about this!" Jay remarked while giving John the one-armed bro hug.

"I'm tellin' ya I know what I saw!" John shot back.

"Said the man who's been mixing rum with beer with vodka..." Ethan chimed in.

"Well, I'm sober now! Shit's crazy. I've gotta go back and see what... where this... I, I dunno!"

Jay reassured him. "Listen, don't worry, we'll figure it out. We'll go back tomorrow and check it out, see what's up. For now, just chill," Jay spied a vulnerable wallflower. "...and watch me work my magic. Take notes fellas. Johnny Depp, Don Juan Demarco."

Jay turned back as he slid on over to her. "What can I say? Some of us just got game..." He did his signature gesture of clapping his hands, thrusting both arms forward and then smoothing the sides of his hair. While the rest watched in amusement as the oddly attractive, bespeckled nerd predictably shot Jay down without the slightest hesitation, John's head sank into the soft back of the welcoming couch and despite the overwhelming aroma of stale beer and cigarettes emanating from the matted red velvet, the white noise of the party fell away, and John drifted into that wonderfully deep sleep that only mild drunkenness can produce.

It always began in the same way. The sounds of someone's labored breathing, running footsteps, the slapping of branches- all set against the backdrop of pitch-black nothingness. Patches of moonlight, viewed through loosely woven burlap, broke the night sky to reveal a thin, uniformed man carrying a toddler wrapped in bed linens in the darkness of a dense, steamy jungle. They stopped and they listened. Suddenly the silence was broken by the whizzing of a thousand spears and arrows. All manner of killing instruments raced towards them through the thick night air, barely missing them, spurring them on.

In the distance across a clearing, a lone bulb shone, illuminating a half-opened door to a rusted steel hanger on what appeared to be a long-abandoned airstrip. He had to make it.

The little guy seemed amused by it all and began waving his arms in the same manner a conductor readies his orchestra. The shitstorm of menacing objects began to bend and twist, missing their intended target, deflected magically somehow by his actions and instead formed a huge, towering pile whose peak disappeared high into the night sky. Only another 200 yards to safety but it was not meant to be. The man's foot became entangled in a complex nest of jungle vines and he toppled to the ground, spilling his precious cargo onto the soft jungle floor. The toddler picked himself up and looked to where the danger lay. Amid this threatening wall of a thousand sharpened steel points, a face appeared. It was that of a woman with long, dark hair, dark skin and kind, expressive eyes. The toddler giggled at the sight and to the horror of the man, ran back to her.

"Mom!?" John gasped.

He looked around only to realize it was that stupid, never-ending dream he always had. For as long as he could remember that scenario would play itself out, an endless tape loop, always stopping at that very moment. He'd even taken to forcing himself back to sleep to continue the dream, to see it to its conclusion, but it never went any further.

Thankfully, no one around him woke, so his less than cool outburst went mercifully without a witness. The apartment was still the disheveled, stinky mess it was when they arrived last night, only with less disheveled, stinky people. He lifted a stranger's hand that had made its final resting place on his thigh and pried himself out from under another partygoer's leg wrapped in a beer-stained tablecloth. At least that's what he hoped it was. He glanced at his phone. It was daylight, which meant that no matter what time it was, it was time to leave - and he was most certainly late once again.

C H A P T E R   4

HATCHING A PLOT

E than and Max leaned against a low brick wall watching the parade of undergrads and their parents making their way across the campus commons. Max took a long draw on his purple vape pipe and produced a white cloud nearly big enough to obscure the banner on the wall behind them that read:

WELCOME PARENTS! HAVE A SAFE AND FUN-FILLED SPRING BREAK!

"He lives," Max said, pointing at John as he jogged in. "Survived his near alien abduction I see."

Ethan smiled and greeted John. "Hey, you, Ok?"

"Shut up." John shot back. They both laughed.

Looking around Ethan remarked, "Remember when our parents used to come?"

"That would be no," John said matter of factly.

"Ahh…shit, sorry," Ethan said. John just laughed.

"I'll adopt you Ferrum," Max offered.

"God knows, you're old enough," John shot back.

"So, what did happen to 'em?" Max asked.

"Not really sure," John said. "They were researchers, in a jungle somewhere in the South Pacific. I was born there, something bad happened and my Uncle took me away, aaaaand...they never came back."

"Something bad? What kind of bad? I mean, did they get eaten by cannabis?"

John laughed and shook his head. "No canni*bals* Max. I don't really know and everyone who might know is very closed-mouthed about it. Every time I bring it up, I get nothing. They probably just stepped on some government toes and became political prisoners or something. I dunno."

Jay ran up, slightly winded. "Hey! Just said goodbye to my parents."

"They do know you're a graduate student, right?" asked Ethan.

"Yeah, why? Anyway, I just might have our ticket out of here for spring break. My Dad's company is doing some goodwill. They're going over to someplace in the middle of the Pacific to feed some babies and build soccer fields for some underprivileged kids. He wanted to know if we'd all go over and teach them the game. It's right on the beach."

"I'm in!" proclaimed Ethan.

"Yessss! Max shouted. "Is that anywhere near that Cargo Cult place? 'Cause we could film-"

"Max! Give it a rest," an exasperated John said.

Jay turned to John. "Hey, listen, the company Lear's only got room for three of us. It's a lot slower but I checked with my dad and I know Aiden is scheduled to head out tomorrow. Can you-"

"Done!" John cut him off. "Say no more - I am *so* there."

"If you head out tomorrow, we'll still probably beat you there. But hey, it'll just give us a chance to chill the beer before you get there,"

Ethan approached John and quietly asked, "Do you want to head back over there? The bar, I mean? Check things out?"

John smiled. "You're a good friend."

"Good friend of a crazy man!" Ethan joked.

Ethan turned down the tunes as they got closer to the Red Witch. "So, what did this guy look like?" asked Ethan.

"Besides ridiculously scary?" John answered. "He was huge! I mean, huge. Had to be pushin' close to seven feet. Everything was big- his head, his hands... and ya know, something was messed up about his hands, but it was dark, and he came at me so fast. I honestly think I was blinded by a touch of panic."

Ethan laughed. "A touch of alcohol maybe?"

"There might have been a bit of that," John smiled. "But how does somebody just disappear into-"

"Well, what is this?" Ethan interrupted. Standing in the alleyway was half the cast of *Men in Black*, all in dark suits at the entrance, examining it. A black van was parked at the curb, its side door slightly ajar, revealing a bank of equipment and a fourth man seated inside. As Ethan and John continued to roll up on the scene, a tall man holding a valise took notice of them.

"Drive! drive! drive!!" yelled John. Ethan looked straight ahead and drove straight past them.

"See? What did I tell you!?" John's eyes were now as big as saucers. "Now the *government* is involved!"

"The government!?" Ethan burst out laughing. "So now I have a crazy *and* paranoid friend." Ethan checked his rearview mirror. "Although I've got to admit, that *is* a little creepy. Guess we're gettin' out of town just in time." John turned to look back and met Ethan's glance with a grimace. It only added to the mystery, giving John even more questions. But if nothing else, it was somewhat vindicating and that made it oddly worth it. "Yeah," he thought, "getting out of town might just be exactly what he needed."

At 58, Gerard Le Muir was the picture-postcard version of a career military officer. His hair was always neat and trimmed, his clothes and shoes impeccable. He had emigrated from France when he was 20, proceeded to join the Army, and had quickly risen through the ranks to Colonel but had stalled somewhere, and frankly, at his age, that was probably as far as he would go. There was a certain amount of resentment that he managed to keep hidden, but every now and then would surface in an unspoken tension and uneasiness for those around him.

When John's parents disappeared, Gerard became John's legal guardian and did the best he could in raising him. As one would imagine he had more of a drill sergeant style of parenting, but all things considered, both John and he had weathered the storm that is childhood well. Gerard was a man of few words and was particularly closed-mouthed about John's biological parents. But John, if nothing else, respected him enough that even at this age, felt compelled to call him and inform him of his new, impromptu travel plans.

Gerard was comfortably seated in an overstuffed leather chair when his phone rang. He raised a finger to interrupt his current conversation.

"Allo!"

"Hey, hi. It's me," John said.

"Calling kind of early, aren't you? Forget about the time difference in Tokyo?" Gerard said.

"Oooh, yeah, sorry, but your military types are up and at 'em at first light, right?"

"How are you boy?"

"I'm good. Hey, listen, if I lose you, I'll call you back later tonight but I'm gonna take a little road trip with the guys."

"Where you off to?" asked Gerard.

"Not entirely sure- Jay's kinda putting this charity thing together but wherever it is it's gonna be sunny. I'm gonna hitch a ride with Aiden... "

"Aiden!? Look, I'll help you out with a ticket if you go commercial but not... "

Thanks, that's OK... He's workin' that route and it's been forever since he and I got together so..."

"Well, I guess it's crazy to think any parents might be coming along to make sure things don't get out of hand."

"Well, Jay's dad... is... sort of... involved in it." John grimaced at his truth-stretching; even pulling the phone away. "As soon as I get more details, I'll ca-"

And with that he crumpled the now empty potato chip bag around the phone and punched the end call button. It bothered him that he was so good at this kind of fakery. It bothered him that he gained that level of skill from having to do it so many times growing up. And so many times Gerard had failed to prove that it even mattered to him.

"John? Hello? Helloooo? Lost him. Must be the long distance...."

Gerard holstered his phone and walked to the window.

"The quiz?" asked Gerard, returning to his conversation.

Professor Wharton returned to his thoughts. "Oh, yeah, the quiz. He got every answer right. Every. Single. One! And in less than three minutes."

The wheels in Gerard's head began to turn. Moving a slat in the blinds he peered out the window and watched as John and his friends walked away.

"They're planning some sort of trip," Gerard said as he made his way to the door. "Aiden is back in the picture. He stopped and turned. They both exchanged a knowing look. "You will keep an eye, won't you?"

"As always," Professor nodded.

As he walked towards the elevators he reached for his phone and scrolled through his contact list. Waiting for his call to be answered, he reached out and impatiently punched the already lit elevator call button several times evoking an abbreviated eye-roll from one of the other waiting faculty members.

"Things are accelerating," he said as he entered the elevator. He turned, faced front, and let his eyes drift to the ceiling. As the doors closed, "No. That ship has sailed. We need to do the same."

CHAPTER 5

MISS EDNA

Weaving his way through the noise and confusion of planes and careening cargo-laden forklifts, John jogged his way over towards the rusty, pale green hanger that for so many years was his childhood home away from home. Inside was a tired 1948 Aero Commander that always seemed to smell of leaking diesel no matter how many repairs were made and how many thunderstorms had washed it. Emblazoned on the side was a bright red, hand painted "Miss Edna" whose story to this day remains a well-kept secret. Running his hand along its underbelly, John hoped that maybe this trip a hint of that story would be revealed.

"I was bloody well gettin' ready to leave without you!" boomed Aiden.

Aiden was, as John's friends portrayed. 60ish, unkempt, spikey greying hair, face like the inside of an old worn catcher's mitt and an accent that drifted somewhere between Cockney English and Crocodile Dundee Australian. He was reminiscent of Keith

Richards- only without the advantages that the Stones' entire body blood transfusions and money would have given him.

"Not a chance and you know it," John replied.

"What makes you so cock-sure?"

"The airport lounge doesn't close for another two hours," John said with a smirk.

"Oh, no!" Aiden corrected him. "I gave all that up a while ago- come to find out it's not good for you ya' know.

"Well how long has that been?" asked John.

"Ooof...gotta' be... well over an hour now." A wry smile formed on his face. "Which reminds me... it's time to take my vitamins."

Aiden reached into his flight bag and threw back a couple of pills and proceeded to wash it down with what looked like cough medicine.

"Don't they usually have labels on those bottles?" asked John. Aiden winked at him.

Some things never changed. But there they were, together again, piloting Miss Edna's rattling parts through the first cloud layer. John wasn't worried. He never was on the many trips of the past and this was just more of the happy same. He somehow knew things would be fine. They always were with Aiden and it was oddly peaceful to him. The headphones reduced the engine roar to a manageable din and gave him the feeling that it was just he and Aiden in their exclusive, private world having another one of their wonderfully private conversations. To the curious teenage John, Aiden had always been the crass Uncle that would fill him in on the real story after the adults had finished spinning their age appropriate BS.

The second cloudbank produced a sizable series of bumps and rattles that managed to dislodge an old photo from the visor. It looked like one of those old black and white photos of Emilia Earhart's search party- a group of squinty-eyed white people in khakis and pith helmets with a group of curious, half-naked, smiling villagers in the background. John picked it up and looked to Aiden to explain.

"Oh! There's a bit a' your family history there, mate. The four of you and the handsome one there? Yours truly."

"It's Wharton!" John shouted. "Was his hair ever not grey?"

He continued to study it when he was startled as the radio crackled with a random, indiscernible voice.

"Ya' got that thing turned up loud enough?", asked John.

"What?"

John just shook his head and smiled.

Aiden turned to John. "Say, does your father know what you lads are up to?"

"You mean Uncle," John corrected.

"Uncle, father, parental unit. The man raised you for pity's sake. Mind you, I'm no fan of that cheese-eating surrender monkey nor he of me but-

"Wait, what?" John burst out laughing at what he had just heard.

"Bloody Frenchman. But ... he might as well be your dad, I mean..."

"Well, it's always been Uncle," John interrupted. "Maybe it's been a respect thing, maybe just a way of keeping his memory alive. My real father, I mean."

"Or maybe he'd rather not claim you," joked Aiden.

"I've been a good guy, not much trouble."

"Yeah, a little too good," Aiden said.

"What's that supposed to mean?"

"Pfft... you know..."

"Nooo, I don't know!" John firmly stated.

"You're serious. What? You never noticed that you're good at everything you try? Like E V E R Y thing? Doesn't that seem the least bit odd to you?"

"No, 'cause I'm not!" a slightly indignant John replied.

"But you NEVER fail!" Aiden said laughing.

"Sure, I do! Plenty!"

"At least not at anything that matters. Mate, I've watched you grow up. I've seen you pull way too many stunts that would have buried anyone else, but you? You're like a cat- you always land on your feet."

"No different than anybody else," John added. Aiden was suddenly serious.

"That's where your wrong mate. Way wrong. You're different. They suspected it from the time you were a baby, that whole levitation thing, from the night we flew you out of the jungle-"

"Wa-wait. We? You? You got us out?" John asked. Aiden was nodding. "No shit," John said in a pensive moment.

Aiden paused, his head down, unsure whether to continue. John looked at him, turned his palms upward, and cocked his head as if to say... "and???"

"I always thought you knew that," Aiden said quietly. He reached in his bag and took another nervous medicinal sip of his cough medicine. "Ahhh, bloody hell... why the hell not?" Aiden muttered to himself.

"I was just buttoning up Miss Edna for the night- oh, she was much prettier then-like me," he said with a wink. "A near-empty bottle of Jack in one hand, the other trying to get the wheels chocked when a busted up Willys comes screaming out the bush. Headed right for us. So, this wanker in fatigues jumps outta that Jeep and pushes his service revolver into my cheek just below me left eye." Aiden pointed to his cheek with a finger pistol hand gesture. "Mad as a bag of ferrets he was, and big too! All the while screamin' about some baby..."

On any other night, the Vanuatu jungle's constant drone of a thousand creature conversations would remain unbroken. But this night was different. There were voices. Angry voices. And not just a few.

They were coming from the torch-lit field office of the research team. Wisps of thick, greasy, black smoke seeped out the windows, the smell of lamp oil and pitch mixed with foreboding permeated the room. John Ferrum, the ruggedly handsome 38-year-old team leader was now seated in its' center, tied tightly to one of the crudely made wooden chairs. For the last three years, he had led the team with the full support and cooperation from the local tribesmen. Some he would even consider friends. The same tribesmen that were now mere inches from his face, screaming at him and taking pot shots with fists and ax handles. Their eyes wild and menacing, their retinas reduced to pinpoints from their deliberate overdosing on Kava. John was struck and thrown to the floor of the dimly lit room, the chair still tied to him. Out of the shadows a figure righted the chair and leaned in to hear the whispers of a now bloodied and gravelly voiced John.

"Gerry? Gerry! They got Miriam and they'll take the boy when they find him- Do not let that happen!"

Before he could utter another word, John was quickly pulled back into the chaos. The yelling, the screaming, punctuated by the disturbing dull thwacks of fists landing on flesh. It was painful to watch but Gerard was completely outnumbered. His was an agonizing triage decision- find the boy and leave John behind. Immediately Gerard scanned the room. No sign of the boy anywhere. But then, from underneath a tattered cot in the far corner of the room, he saw the momentary reflection of a torch in two little blue eyes that fearfully peered out from underneath it. In the distraction, he was able to gather him up in a dirty bed sheet and made his way to the back window. His mind raced, desperate to see any other options. Stopping momentarily, he gathered his wits and strength and with one, final snap decision, leapt through the crude wooden shutters and fell out of the window.

Despite the raucous howling and screaming of the villagers, the sound of the breaking shutters had somehow drawn the attention of the interrogators. They looked out the broken window just in time to see the back of Gerard's sweat drenched khaki shirt disappear into the foliage carrying their ultimate prize. Suddenly untold numbers were in hot pursuit and all manner of primitive jungle weaponry began whizzing past Gerard's head. Clutching the toddler tighter still, he raced into the darkness of the dense jungle towards the only hope of safety, the lone dim light of the airfield. He stopped at the edge of the clearing, hiding from the crazed hunters behind a giant yucca. His lungs, now at the brink of exploding, tore at his chest, his heart pounding so hard he swore his enemies could hear it. "Breathe! Breathe through the nose" he warned himself, struggling to control his breathing, He held his breath momentarily and listened for the determined warriors. They were getting closer. Before him was the last three hundred yards, an entire football field without a single bit of cover. Once he committed, he'd be wide open to whatever death punch was waiting to swoop in and end his life and the life of John's only son. One last gamble, one last roll of the dice. Gerard's eyes narrowed, his jaw tightened and with one last gulp of humid night air, he bolted for the hanger.

"Run!! Just keep running!" he thought. He should have been filled with fear but there was no room for it. It had been pushed out the moment he took his first step onto the field by his overwhelming need to survive. Suddenly arrows began to appear. sticking out of the ground in back of him, in front of him, and to the side. He felt the sting in his left leg as a feathery spear caught the cuff of his pant leg, grazing his calf. It stuck in the soft ground spinning him around but like a good offensive receiver, managed a complete 360 and kept moving towards the goal post, never once letting go of the ball.

He managed to make it to the hanger, pressing himself up against the metal building. From the corner Gerard could see Aiden being confronted by a soldier in fatigues forcefully motioning him to the cockpit. Some of the warrior hunters were still coming across the field determined to strip the Colonel of his stolen prize. In a moment their torchlight would expose him but the soldier noticed them coming. Shielding his eyes from the glaring light bulb, he drew his weapon and popped off a round, hitting one of the savages squarely in the chest.

Here was his chance. The immediate threat had been neutralized and an idling plane beckoned with it's cargo doors wide open, sitting just 15 yards in front of him. He had no idea where it was going but anywhere was better than where he was. Gerard and his precious bed linens snuck aboard the aircraft and as luck would have it, it taxied and took off into the relative safety of the night sky.

"Well, that explains a lot-this dream- ever since I was a kid..." John said. "So, when did you realize we were on board?" he asked.

"Right about when your uncle threw my gun-toting guest out the left cargo bay," Aiden said matter of factly. John was taken aback and looked at Aiden in astonishment.

"What?!" Aiden said in mock indignation. "He threw him a parachute pack on his way out the door. Or a knapsack filled with MRE's- was never entirely sure, it was dark," Aiden continued to eye John. "It's just bloody impolite to shove a 45 up someone's nose..." John shook his head in disbelief.

"So where exactly was this? I know it was some sort of jungle, somewhere in this corner of the Pacific, but no one would ever say for sure."

"And they never will, mate," Aiden shot back. " They don't want you to know. It's too dangerous."

"Dangerous? Wait, wait. Dangerous? And who are 'they'? Aiden sighed and shook his head trying to decide whether to go on. "Come on, spill, I wanna know!" John demanded.

Aiden lowered his voice. "There are people that would kill me if they knew I was talking to you about this."

"Who?" John asked.

"People!" Aiden yelled. "Just...people, OK?" John held up his hands in surrender.

Aiden continued, "Your father-"

"Uncle," John corrected him.

"No! your real father now. Your father had some umm...." Aiden searched for the words, "abilities that western people couldn't understand. And what western people can't understand? They fear."

"Why?"

"Power. Money, Influence. Anything that threatens the status quo is cause for fear for them. When they couldn't get him to cooperate, they uhhh.... arranged things, turning everyone against him. So, the tribe ended up banishing him to a remote part of the island. If they can keep him away from the people..."

"What abilities are we talking about here? Alchemy, the Fountain of Youth, what?"

Aiden shook his head. "Something far more valuable and far more frightening to them." He took a long, contemplative breath. "He could cause things to occur that would defy natural laws." Aiden paused, allowing that to sink in. "It was spooky, actually. He bloody well didn't make it any easier on himself tellin' 'em that he was nothing special, it wasn't him. He even told them the stuff he was doin' anybody could do. That was the real fear. He told them it was- what'd he call it?" Aiden paused, looking to the tattered ceiling for the memory. "That's it! The immutable law of believing. Believing is receiving, he used to always say. He said you could even find it in the good book. They all thought he was lying-there's the uncooperative part - and that it had to be some sort of complicated formula or something that he was hiding."

"Oh... So, when this plays itself out, their real concern was a bunch of guys doing the same thing gets beyond their control," John interrupted.

"Exactly," affirmed Aiden. "And that's the name of the game. Control."

John was still trying to put it all together. "Alright, but why would this be dangerous for me?"

"Because you mate, might have the same thing your dad did. And from what I've seen, you've got it bad. The idea of you two... well...." Aiden trailed off. " They've been workin' since day one to keep you distracted, keep you from figuring this all out... then doing something with it."

"They don't know anyth-"

"Oh yes they do!!" Aiden interrupted with such force he began coughing. "They know everything! They think you're the key to," coughing, "well, you and your ability are the only thing that can stop them from getting absolute power. And they will do anything...and I mean *anything* to make sure you don't mess up their plan. That's why we've been hiding you all these..."

Aiden holds up his hand and tries to squelch his coughing spasm. John's hands grabbed his head..

"Hiding me!? Why am I just now finding all this out!?" he barked. "Why hasn't my uncle told me? Why haven't *you* told me Aiden? How many times have I flown with you and you're just now mentioning it!? Did it ever occur to you I might want to know... something about my father, my life!? And Goddammit! Who are *THEY!!*

He glared at Aiden. There were so many questions bombarding John's mind all at once and from every conceivable direction- what abilities? What people? An entire secret life gone unexplained and the life they were talking about? Was his! Absolutely crazy.

Aiden was at a loss for a reason, any reason that John would understand and accept. It wasn't supposed to be him, he wasn't supposed to be tasked with filling John in on his destiny but at this point...

"They've got watchers," Aiden said. "Good watchers and bad watchers and- Shite!" A loud thump and smoke began pouring from left engine number two. It sputtered, briefly returned to life, and sputtered one final time before dying completely.

"Ahhh for the love of- we're gonna have to set her down. Bollocks! Get me that map behind the seat. Whaaat a bag o' wank this is!" exclaimed Aiden.

As John fumbled to find the map, more and more alarm bells filled the cabin. Aiden, usually cool under these circumstances, quickly graduated from concerned to full-blown terror.

"The map, the map. the map!" he shouted.

John suddenly paused, lowered his head into his hands, and exhaled. Just as suddenly he raised his head and said, "How 'bout there?" pointing to a large island straight ahead as it came into view on the horizon just as they cleared a cloudbank. Aiden's shoulders slumped in relief.

"Sure." Aiden burst into laughter. "An airstrip. Perfect. Of course. See?

"See what? John asked.

"You're doing it, what we were just talking about? John appeared puzzled.

"Aaaaand, you don't see how you just about pulled that out of your arse, right?" Aiden continued. "We need an airstrip. There it is!" Aiden looked back to his map. "Bloody hell, it's not even on my map!" he exclaimed. "Shite!"

CHAPTER 6

THE WELCOMING COMMITTEE

The welcome sight of the dirt airstrip ahead was still a challenge for Aiden. Engine number two had long since given up the ghost and keeping Miss Edna aloft and on track with the use of only one engine was not only nerve-wracking, but a true test of his piloting skills and physical endurance. With plumes of thick, oily, black smoke spewing out of the engine cowl, a wobbly Miss Edna served up a rough landing, but any landing you can walk away from...

They taxied over to the lone hanger, quickly shut her down, and jumped out to get a better look. Standing in the shadows of the open hangar was what appeared to be the resident mechanic. Stepping away from his beat-up Cessna, he slowly wiped his greasy hands while suspiciously eyeing his new and uninvited guests. He was a big guy, massively big guy with rather garish features but the hope was that he spoke at least *some* English.

"Aye mate, are you a sight for sore eyes! Don't know how, but you just popped up in the nick of time." Aiden shot a look at John. "Where exactly are we?"

Dead silence. The mechanic stood motionless, staring at them. "Well then. Seems we lost oil pressure and started burnin' what was left. Just a clogged line maybe?" Aiden suggested. "If I could just borrow that crescent wrench for-"

Without a word, the mechanic dropped his wrench, turned, and walked towards the back office in the rear of the hanger. Aiden looked at John. "Fun guy." Who pissed in his cornflakes?"

He reached down to pick up the wrench and noticed that John was standing wide-eyed, motionless- almost frozen.

"What?" Aiden asked. "What?" Staring towards the back of the hanger John spoke carefully.

"A couple of nights ago...something happened. A guy who looked just like Mr. Happy here... he, ughh..." Aiden could sense John's reluctance. His eyes narrowed as he waited for John to continue.

"Ahh, this is nuts...I don't even believe..."

"Try me," Aiden quickly shot back.

"He came at me, in the dark and just as he was gettin' ready to land one on me..." John hesitated. "He got sucked up into thin air. Vanished! Gone! Just like that!" he said, snapping his finger. "I know this sounds absolutely nuts-"

"Does this end with you on your back?"

"Yeah! Yeah, it did- how'd you know?" Aiden grimaced and turned his attention to the oil-spattered engine. "How did you know?" John asked again.

"Jump in the cockpit, lad."

Silently proceeding with the repair all the while shooting glances at John, Aiden signaled him to try and start it. The engine cranked and surprisingly fired up. A tad rough at first but it was running. Off in the distance, an olive drab military transport appeared at the edge of the tree line and was approaching them at a good clip.

"Somebody's in a hurry," muttered Aiden. He motioned for John to stay put. John slid the left cockpit window open.

"Bad time to ask, but what *are* we carrying?"

Aiden raised an eyebrow. "Rule number one- no names. Rule number two- never open the package."

Excitedly pointing and wagging his finger at Aiden, "! Frank Martin. I love that movie! But really, what-"

Holding his finger to his lips Aiden's gaze narrowed. "Veeeery important stuff- top, top secret. Guard it with your life!"

"Hey, we are not done yet," John reminded him. "How did you know?"

Aiden turned to face the approaching party placing his hands confidently on his hips. He looked back at John reassuringly, breaking into his signature 'I'm powerful yet friendly' toothy grin. Both knew it was total BS, but it had worked in the past and they were hoping it would work now. Aiden, however, knew these guys didn't just happen on the scene - they had been summoned.

The truck's squeaking brakes could be heard even through the thick cockpit glass. John watched as five or six sweaty locals piled out from under the olive drab canvas and hastily formed a sloppy formation. Their uniforms were hardly that. It was as if they had fallen into a Goodwill box and simply put on the first thing that fit. The scene reminded John of those old grainy newspaper photos he'd seen, captured by journalists during rare jungle meetings with Che Guevara and his loyal compadres.

Unable to hear the conversation taking place between Aiden and what he presumed to be the commanding officer, John watched carefully, trying to get an idea of what exactly was going on.

After some discussion two men approached Aiden, grabbed him under each arm and escorted him towards the hanger. Aiden looked back at John. Rolling his eyes, he mouthed, "It's OK" and followed up with the BJ mime- tongue against cheek, fist to mouth making John laugh. It's what he loved about Aiden. Even in difficult situations he always managed to find the humor. Not always the most prudent thing to do mind you, but always funny.

Two of the soldiers boarded Miss Edna from the back cargo hatch and began a lackluster search of the rear cargo bay. John stepped out of the plane and was met by three menacing paramilitary guys. The biggest of the three put his hand out preventing him from going any further.

"Your friend, he carry contraband?" he asked in a thick, Bislamic accent.

"No!" John shot back.

"Your friend poacher? You poacher? You have drugs?"

Exasperated, John's head lowered as he let out an audible sigh. "Nope," he said. "Kahore i roto i reira anake te kaitaka paruparu i te tūroro Ebola kawea matou. Here, he titiro..."

(Nothing in there except dirty linens from the Ebola patients we transported. Here, have a look...)

John turned his head away as he opened the hatch, hoping to hide the look of sheer shock and amazement that was now written all over his face. Suddenly he's able to speak Bislama? Fluently? The three soldiers nervously glanced at each other and slowly backed away.

Suddenly their semi-autos were pointed at him. John wondered if they routinely shot sorcerers but quickly realized the Ebola comment had had more impact when the other two men ran out of the aircraft holding their hand over their mouths.

"Whiwhi hoki koe i runga i taua waka rererangi! Na! Ka tangohia e ia koe atu te motu!" yelled the biggest one. (You get back on that plane! Now! He will take you off the island!) He pointed towards a short, sweaty midget of a man wearing a perpetual grin.

"Easy! just chill guys," John looked to ease the tension. "All I want to know-"

"Is where you are going?" a man interrupted. He was white, dressed in contemporary civilian clothes and, best of all, spoke fluent English. "Of course! I'm so sorry," He said, pulling on the brim of his imported straw fedora. "I must apologize for my men. They lack some of the umm... refinements... customarily afforded to western travelers such as yourself." He removed his sunglasses and cleaned them with a monogrammed handkerchief. "We must unfortunately detain your friend. You see, we've received word of a plane fitting this description involved in some unsavory black-market activities. He will have to stay until we clear him and this aircraft. A mere formality, I'm sure."

"Sure," John said. "I think your boys here just cleared it."

Without exception, all the wide-eyed men began nodding convincingly.

"In that case..." he then summoned the sweaty, smiley Mini-Me. "I've dispatched my finest pilot to take you straight away to Vanuatu.

There you will have many options while you await your friend. Have a safe flight, Mr. Ferrum."

"How did you know my name?" John asked.

He stiffened, momentarily flustered but quickly recovered. "The manifest. You're listed on the manifest."

He abruptly turned and walked towards the hanger.

That was odd, thought John. The manifest? Aiden hadn't bothered with a manifest since he left that fledgling little start-up called FedEx. John looked over towards the hanger where Aiden stood with his 'captors'. As usual, by this point, Aiden was regaling the men with stories of his far-off, drunken adventures, and the men appeared to be enjoying every minute of it. Aiden waved at John and gestured for him to go.

"Go, go ahead, go" he mouthed. John gathered up his things, turned and acknowledged the over-smiling pilot, and clamored back into the Nav seat of Miss Edna. The pilot fired her up and began to turn her upwind. As soon as John's line of sight to Aiden was interrupted, the man in the straw fedora slowly nodded towards the men surrounding Aiden. The smiles and laughter quickly disappeared, and the biggest one sucker-punched Aiden, knocking him out cold. They caught him before he even had a chance to hit the ground and carried him like an old, rolled-up area rug into the darkness of the hanger.

The still sputtering Miss Edna did little to invoke confidence in John who eyed the new pilot with suspicion. Something just didn't add up and John was unconvinced that leaving Aiden behind for the last leg of the journey was such a good idea.

"Do you speak English?" John asked. No response. He stared unflinchingly ahead, all the while sporting that creepy, pasted-on smile. John noticed his bulky uniform and wondered why on earth would anyone choose to wear that in this sweltering, sticky, tropical blast furnace. He wondered if perhaps the little guy had started this morning a normal-sized person and like a snowman had simply melted.

"We are headed to Vanuatu, correct?" John asked, "Vanuatu?" No response. John looked out the window and wondered out loud, "Isn't the sun supposed to be there? And not there?"

The otherwise catatonic pilot locked eyes with John. He stared an uncomfortably long time without blinking even as sweat ran down his round face. John swallowed hard, licking his lips and yet there was no spit left to moisten them. His body tensed, sensing the unspoken danger before his mind could calculate it. Something was coming. But what? Without warning, the little spawn of Satan suddenly cranked the yoke for all it's worth to the left. Miss Edna groaned in protest as she did her best to carry out such a violent command and responded by entering into a series of tight, vomit-inducing barrel rolls. Luckily, John had been strapped in, avoiding any serious injury as everything began flying around the cabin. It was not unlike someone's bratty sister having a temper tantrum and upending the kitchen junk drawer on his head. The plane leveled out and John looked up at the pilot who was now standing next to him motioning for him to head to the rear of the plane.

"I'm not going anywhere-" John's objection was cut short when he noticed the matte-finished reflection of the barrel of a small handgun protruding from the sleeve of the little guy's coat. "Whoa! alright, alright-"

BANG!

CHAPTER 7

FLYING LESSONS

"So, this is what it's like to be shot," John thought. "It doesn't hurt... "Oh, wait a minute- yes it does, it absolutely does!!"

He frantically grabbed at his chest, just above his heart. "God this *really* hurts!" he thought. "Wait, there's no blood. Am I bleeding? There's no blood." There was a small tear in his shirt. He felt a bump and instinctively pulled it away. It was a dart. A small, crude, handmade dart. "Oh, OK, " he thought, somehow relieved that he hadn't been shot shot. Just darted like a National Geographic lion of the Serhengeti. His attention returned to the little guy. "It's gonna take a lot more than this to stop me from kicking your pint-sized ass," he proclaimed.

He lunged towards the pilot and immediately face planted onto the dirty, junk-covered floor. Someone had replaced his legs with rubber ones so, to anyone other than Gumby, they were now pretty much useless. His vision was beginning to follow suit, as if he'd mistakenly put on someone else's glasses. But he could see enough to notice that the creepy smile was still there and why that little monkey's flight suit had been so bulky. There was a parachute beneath it. John's eyes grew wide, his mouth dropped open in terror as it suddenly dawned on him what that meant. That three foot menace had no plans of sticking around to finish the flight.

The pilot then proceeded to calmly pull the rusty cotter pin from the center wheel and removed the yoke. He reached for the red emergency cockpit escape latch, struggling to get it to work. Still on the floor, John realized what was about to happen and had the presence of mind to wrap his arm around one of the co-pilot's seat support legs. The latch released. In an instant, the cockpit's glass surround was suddenly gone. The wind had caught it and cleanly ripped it from the fuselage almost taking his pint-sized head with it. He, the yoke, and anything else that wasn't tied down was sucked out of the plane and disappeared into the blue sky.

The engine noise, the rushing wind were all amplified without the cockpit glass and just added to John's complete and utter confusion. And whatever was on the tip of that dart certainly wasn't helping matters. He laid there, alone, frozen, in disbelief trying to sort things out.

"What just happened!?" he thought. But there clearly was no time for that. Miss Edna's nose dipped. She began to slowly plummet towards the turquoise water below. He had to do something, and he had to do it now. He closed his eyes and took a long breath. It was what he always did, since he was a kid to center himself, to calm the nervousness, to tamp down the fear just before he took *any* action. He exhaled, pulled himself to his knees, and reached blindly under the tattered seat. His hand found his salvation- a pair of long forgotten, rusted vice grips. He pulled himself up into the captain's seat, strapped himself in, all the while fighting the mounting fog that was rolling over his brain. He shook his head and screamed to startle himself awake. Even the simple act of opening the jaws of the vice grips now took a monumental effort. He managed to attach them to where the yoke used to be. It worked, sort of.

Struggling, he was able to bring her nose up, leveling out into a slow, 180-degree arc that positioned him in line with a distant land mass barely visible on the horizon. What he was going to do once he got there was uncertain. But whatever happened, he figured it had to be better than having it happen in the middle of the Pacific.

"Tank, I need a pilot program for a B212 helicopter- hurry." If only, he thought. He laughed out loud and finished it. "Trinity, *The Matrix*."

"That would have been obvious," he said to himself. "Ethan would have gotten tha..." He was drifting.

"Concentrate!" he shouted to no one while shaking his head. There were trees ahead, coming at him way too fast and dangerously close.

Off in the distance, John could see his only hope for a landing. It was a long, wide, unobstructed stretch of white sand beach on the opposite side of the island. With his vision impaired it was hard for him to tell how far that was, but one thing was for sure- he needed to clear the trees first or he'd never make it.

He struggled to stay conscious, pep-talking his way through each action he took. "Come on!! Get it together, just pull the stick back, you can do this!" he shouted, shaking his head to keep his own pilot light lit.

What John had failed to realize was that ever since Tattoo had jumped out with yoke in hand, he had been slowly losing altitude and was now left with a mere 185 feet between him and the water. The product of a prehistoric volcano, the island he was attempting to vault rose dramatically at the shoreline- nearly a hundred feet from the seafloor. Add to that the jungle that carpeted it, John had officially run out of room.

"Shit! Too low!" he suddenly realized. At 210 knots the trees were now racing towards him. Marshalling every adrenaline-fueled ounce of strength he had left, he wrapped both hands around the stick, arched his back and using his body weight, threw himself against the seat back. In the midst of all this he somehow remembered what Aiden had said to him about lift. "Planes are like giant teeter-totters. Put some weight in the back and the bloody nose will go right up." In a last-ditch effort, he grabbed Aiden's old surplus radio and threw it towards the rear of the aircraft. He laughed as it succeeded in nudging Miss Edna's nose up a bit.

He continued pulling back as the constant sound of alarm bells and a badly misfiring engine were replaced by the thunderous noise of branches breaking against aluminum. But Miss Edna, God bless her, refused to give up. She somehow managed to clear the first hilltop and gained a bit of clearance as the small, natural valley dipped below her. But her hedge clipping had cost her. Her remaining engine's shroud had been pierced by an errant branch and was now pouring out thick, black smoke.

"Ugh! What next?" thought John out loud. Fate took no time in answering as a loud, slapping sound against the fuselage filled the cockpit. The scraping branches had not only damaged his remaining good engine, but they had also severed the cabling whose purpose was controlling the rudder and were now dangerously flailing about. Fighting back the panic at this new problem, he welcomed the sight of the expansive beach a short 2 miles directly ahead of him. Just 2 miles, that's all he needed.

"Ok, we can't go left, we can't go right but we're level," he said trying to put a positive spin on it. "We still have power-" He hadn't so much as finished his sentence when the left engine coughed, wheezed, and died. The propeller didn't even slow to stop. It made a high-pitched metal on metal grinding squeal and simply seized.

"We still have *some* power." His speech was now beginning to slur. In his heart of hearts, he knew that some power was probably not enough power. Ever the optimist however...

"We can glide," he told himself. That would have been true were it not for the tops of the taller trees that began to pop and scrape on Miss Edna's underbelly causing her to lose what precious little altitude she had left. Unbeknownst to John, his hearing by this time had ceased to be a reliable source of information and without it, he determined that NOW was a good time to drop the landing gear.

"Ladies and gentlemen, as we begin our final descent, please return your seat backs to.... your tray tables... to their full... upright.... positions..." He was delirious at this point and fading fast.

The decision to lower his gear was a fateful one. Up ahead, rising above any other tree in the entire jungle canopy, stood a lone, vine-covered tree that was easily a good 15 feet taller than the rest. It stood as a beacon, drawing Miss Edna in and her lowered gear was a grappling hook in search of something to latch onto.

A perfect loop in an enormous vine caught her nose gear and true to the law of physics, when the front suddenly stopped, the back kept going, flipping her on her back.

After a metal-on-metal groan or two, it was suddenly eerily quiet as Miss Edna came to rest upside down, lodged in the thick, green canopy high above the jungle floor. John was enjoying his own sudden serenity in the form of unconsciousness. Seems the drug had finally taken its full effect, and this was as good a place as any to take a much-needed nap.

CHAPTER 8

I'M NOT JOHN FRUM

Life beneath the canopy was the same as it ever was. The ever-present smell of campfire and damp earth from the daily rains filled the air as it had for hundreds, if not thousands of years. Everyone had their routine, even if that routine were to do nothing at all. The men hunted and foraged for food and the women prepared whatever the men were lucky enough to bring back.

There was a peacefulness in that sameness. A rare peacefulness that passed a modern world's understanding.

That routine would be broken today. It started when the jungle's normal, noisy soundtrack fell suddenly silent. It was a stillness that stopped everyone and everything in its tracks. Instinct screamed at them - everyone's head tilted, listening, waiting, watching.

Suddenly the silence was broken with a tremendous roar of something otherworldly skimming the treetops. It was monstrously big, shiny, and blocked out part of the sun briefly as it sailed past them from above. The women hurriedly gathered the little ones and herded them into the safety of their thatched-roofed huts. All the able-bodied men quickly retrieved their weapons before racing off in the direction of the beast's path, a thin line of black smoke leading the way. The hunt was on for this terrifying creature and they would never allow it to get away.

The tribesmen were traveling the well-worn pathways at breakneck speed when the apparent leader of the hunting party raised his right arm holding his long spear skyward, signaling them to stop. The sound and smoke of the winged creature they had been pursuing had dissipated and the uncertain group now awaited his direction. He set his spear down and in a grand gesture, fell to his knees sniffing the ground, rubbing the reddish dirt between his palms. He rose, tilted his head back, and with arms outstretched, closed his eyes. Rubbing his soiled hands on his eyes and ears he took several long, exaggerated breaths and delivered two sharp raps on the ground with the butt end of his feather and bone spear. He then silently ran off, veering towards the ancient ash pits, his band of warriors left to hurriedly catch up to him.

They stopped as they reached the first ash pit. It was a large, diamond-shaped pit, the result of many dreadful eruptions of Mount Yasur, and the bright white ash stood in stark contrast to the mottled, green backdrop that surrounded it. The foliage so lush and thick that it blotted out most of the sun. What little sunlight it did allow, came down in occasional knife blades of filtered, ethereal light that gave it the look of an ancient, alien temple. It was the land of the Great Spirits, invoking both reverence and trepidation in each fierce, war-painted warrior.

The entire pit was surrounded by a massive, exposed root system with some of the roots as large as trees themselves. Rising from those roots was possibly the largest tree in the entire jungle. Its bark was the color of a new cabernet and a texture reminiscent of shredded wheat, certainly different from any of the other surrounding trees. It was massive and that was a good thing because just 135 feet up, completely hidden from view, was a heavy, cargo-laden 1948 Aero Commander nestled in its branches with it's now semi-coherent pilot dangling upside down from his worn and faded seat harness.

John slowly blinked, stinging sweat rolled down his neck, past his chin and into the corners of his eyes. His body feeling as if it had been beaten with a pillowcase filled with loose change, he took inventory of what hurt- his head, his back, every appendage while his shirt tail hung in front of him covering his face. Moving it out of the way revealed such a strange world about him. Something was amiss. His vision wasn't right. Everything had been turned upside down.

"Possible injury from the crash?" he thought. Reaching to his waist he struggled to get his seat harness undone. At the same time Aiden's spare radio, initially thrown from the crash, finally let go from its treetop perch and crashed through the trees, landing some 50 feet behind the skittish hunting party. Already nervous, the group swung around to face this new emerging threat. With weapons poised to strike, they began to slowly move towards it, humming and buzzing for some unknown reason like a newly disturbed hornets' nest.

By the time a hung-over John figured out that his vision wasn't upside down, rather he was, it was too late. He was free falling towards the earth, grazing a haphazard branch or two along the way. and made a desperate but unsuccessful attempt of clinging to them.

It did however serve to flip him 180 degrees and he was now at least plummeting feet first with just a wee bit less speed. He hit the ash pit like an Olympic diver producing an amazingly miniscule dust splash. Upon hearing the commotion, the hunting party executed a perfectly choreographed group heel spin and freeze that would have made a Broadway producer weep. For the first time, their leader wore a genuine look of confusion with just a slight touch of fear that even a fierce warrior's painted face had trouble hiding. They had heard the sounds and knew where they had come from. But there was nothing there. Just a slight wisp of dusty "smoke" from the ash pit's center. The leader cautiously approached, studying, sniffing, looking for any signs of movement. Finally convinced there was none, he turned and walked back towards the group.

It had been just long enough for the group's tensed shoulders to relax when John, like a spawning salmon in an Alaskan river, suddenly shot out of the ash pit, desperately gasping for air. He leapt from the pit with such force that he threw himself out of it and onto its shoreline, nearly landing at the warrior leader's feet. The leader jumped back and screamed like a 10-year-old girl finding a spider in her hair. John quickly stood, now completely white from head to toe, ash filling his eyes and ears. He bent over, with his hands on his knees, shaking his head, trying to catch his breath. His phone fell out of his upper shirt pocket and as he went to pick it up, noticed 20 sets of fear-filled eyes staring at him from the edge of the dimly lit jungle. John's hands instinctively shot up in surrender and let out a startled scream. The fearless leader mimicked him screaming once again and throwing his hands into the air as well. It was a perfect remake of Drew Barrymore discovering ET in the closet full of stuffed animals.

Somehow the alarm on his phone went off and, while trying to silence it, managed to light the flashlight instead. The natives cowered in fear, their voices reduced to a murmur, and one by one began to kneel before him.

John stood wide-eyed, motionless, trying to squelch his panic. "What is this!?" he thought. He slowly lowered his arms. A single beam of light shone down on him through a crack in the green ceiling. He was David of Florence's Galleria Dell'Accademia, the quintessential heavenly vision found in so many religious paintings-just, you know, with cargo pants. The leader, with his now shaking spear pointed at him, slowly approached him. By this time John's vision was seriously blurred and he shook his head vigorously to clear it. At precisely the same time, Aiden's spare radio crackled behind them with static and an indistinguishable voice. "Magic!" they thought, the group recoiling once again.

The group began to gather their courage as John wobbled, and with weapons pointed threateningly, slowly approached him again. Now desperately trying to hold on to consciousness, John fell to his knees and tried once again to shake his head in hopes the distant magic radio would speak and ward them off. It remained silent. When only mere inches away from being skewered, a booming voice rang out.

"Mutu!"

"Stop!"

Suddenly pieces of cargo began dropping from the canopy, surrounding the warriors. There it was. The irrefutable proof. The shocked natives knelt reverently once again, finally convinced he was indeed magic. But John never saw it, having finally succumbed to the venomous dart and was now flat on his back and out cold.

It was hot. Sticky, stagnant, Louisiana-in-July-hot inside the bure' and there lying on an elevated, single bed of palm fronds was John's nearly naked body. Surrounding him were the small bits and pieces recovered from Miss Edna and a number of Aiden's personal items that had fallen from her open cockpit. They had bathed him removing all remnants of the chalky, white ash, and dressed his many scrapes and cuts with a pasty yellow salve. All except his face. There, someone had taken great care to create an angelic, kabuki white face with black lips and incredibly detailed eyes painted on the backs of his eyelids. It was drawn in such a way that the eyes seemed to be looking at you no matter where you were. It gave him a very peaceful albeit creepy, attentive look even as he continued his dart-induced coma.

It had been nearly a week since his impromptu treetop landing, and he drifted in and out of consciousness the entire time. His only memory was that of short, hazy views of a beautiful young woman's face, the face of an angel, peering down while compassionately caring for him. That vision became the compelling force that enabled him to finally awaken fully. His eyes fluttered and then, with great effort, opened wide for the first time.

His first glimpse of his new world was not that of an angel, but that of Sam's face, less than an inch from his and sniffing him. Sam, who was somewhere between 70 and 170 (suffice to say no one can remember a day when Sam wasn't old) had a face that more closely resembled that of an old, leather seat cushion from a well-worn parlor chair with bright expressive eyes and a permanent toothy smile. Sam had a large, pink foam finger that he proudly wore on his head. In another E.T. and Drew Barrymore moment, John recoiled in horror and surprise as did Sam, knocking most of the carefully placed artifacts to the floor.

"Tangohia te reira atu! Hoki te karauna ki a ia!" yelled Heylia, Sams youngest granddaughter.

"Take it off! Return the crown to him!" Sam respectfully bowed, removed the stadium finger from his head, and carefully offered it to John in a manner one would expect if one were presenting the crown jewels. John motioned no and for the first time looked around him. There were hundreds of novelty trinkets surrounding his shrine-like bed. That, and copious bowls of never-before-seen fruit.

Sam's smile had returned, and he was enthusiastically nodding as he asked, "Ko koe Hoani Frum, Ae?" John's eyes narrowed in confusion. Almost immediately Sam grimaced and switched to broken English.

"You are John Frum? Yes?" John studied Sam's face trying to clear the cobwebs. Slowly it sunk in.

"No. No, John Ferrum."

"From America." Sam was still nodding.

"Yes, but..." John ran his fingers through his hair and winced as he touched a tender spot. Sam and his granddaughter Heylia turned, wide-eyed and smiling at one another.

"See!? What I tell? John Frum!" an ecstatic Sam concluded as he pounded his cane into the hard, clay floor. He looked heavenward with palms uplifted in thanks.

"Ferrum. John Ferrum," John emphasized.

"Yes. Yes. Yes," still nodding, still smiling. "You. Have. Returned." Tears were now beginning to fill his eyes and Heylia reached over to console him. John still trying to grasp what was happening,

"What? Oh... no.... uh... oh wow ...it's uh, a mistake. I'm-"

"I have waited...so long!" Sam exclaimed. "Every night at airfield looking to sky...but I knew! I knew... you would see lights, and plane... and you come!" Young Heylia turned to Sam and reassured him.

"Things be good now." She turned to John, "His legs be heal now and-"

"Oh... wait uh... I'm really not...him," John interrupted. John realized that Sam's gaze had drifted to something behind him, and he cautiously turned to see what it was. Hanging directly behind John was Aiden's SpongeBob, Square Pants bathrobe. They had retrieved it from the wreckage, placed it on display, and adorned it with candles and more bowls of unrecognizable sacrificial fruit. Sam seemed transfixed by it.

"If I could just touch-" Sam looked longingly at it.

"It's just a goofy robe! And I'm not-"

Sam wasn't listening and began to reach towards it. "One touch and my legs will be-"

WHACK!

"You not touch Messiah's sacred garment!!" an elderly woman recoiled her long stick readying it for another smackdown.

John's head dropped. "Ahh Geez! Listen..."

Sam was still smiling and nodding. "We go now. Take you to airfield, Yes?"

"Later grandfather, later. He must rest," Heylia said.

"I have to find out about my friend and-"

"Who friend?" Sam interrupted.

"Uhh, his name is Aiden. He's-"

The room exploded in unison, "Aiden! Aiden!!" Everyone was smiling and nodding, repeating his name.

"You know him?" John asked. Everyone in the room was now laughing.

"He say to give you Kava," the elderly woman told him. "Kava take away the sick, John Frum."

John was excited. And hopeful. "So, he was here!?"

"Yes," the elderly woman confirmed. "He come back for you. No worry."

"Yes. Yes." Sam was still grinning and nodding. "Thank you, John Frum."

"I AM NOT JOHN FRUM!!" an exasperated John shouted. Sam was shaking his head, laughing, and shaking a scolding finger at him.

"You... you make such joke... John Frum!"

John closed his eyes and let his head fall back in sheer frustration. Still laughing, Sam turned and hobbled towards the door on what must have been two badly crippled legs. He turned every couple of steps to deliver a series of genuflecting bows, all the while singing a broken English version of *'God Bless America.'*

"God bless Amereekah, land that I loaf..."

CHAPTER 9

PARTYING WITH MARCO

John bolted upright, startled out of his sleep by the rustle of several women suddenly entering his bure'. He still hadn't quite adapted to this new, utopian way of life where most threats, at least the human kind, had been all but eliminated and he still tended to react as if he was back in his low-rent apartment at school. The nakedness was another feature that always took him by surprise at first. Equally surprising, however, was how quickly he had become comfortable with it, the naturalness of it, and how logical it all seemed. At least for others. He laughed at his own odd sense of disappointment at finding out that every teenage boy's dream of being surrounded by naked women was not really sexy at all but far too natural and well, pure.

"You guys have a Forever 21, a mall, or maybe... ya' know, you could pick up some yoga pants and a flattering top or something... "

The girls innocently oblivious to both his language and his humor reacted as they always did- by simply giggling and nodding, not understanding a single word. Just as well John thought.

"I guess not. OK, what are we doin'?" John rubbed his hands together in anticipation. They approached him and stripped him of all his clothing. "Alright, this is a good start," he said. They were smiling and seemed utterly fascinated by his white skin. John smiled in return and said facetiously, "Why yes, I do work out a bit."

He quickly realized their fascination was not with his hard-earned, stellar definition or his pigment-less skin but rather his beat-up, khaki cargo pants and the many zippered and buttoned pockets covering them. They began going through each pocket, delighting in the little treasures discovered in each one. His Swiss Army knife, a few coins, bills, some Q-tips, his keys. They would examine each find and discuss its presumed use. John sat back, enjoying the girls' chatter and fascination of the simplest of things. Why didn't the ordinary things in his life do the same for him? Why do people in his culture only have excitement for the *next* thing?

They stood him up and had him assume the DaVinci pose- feet slightly apart, arms outstretched perpendicular to the body with palms facing forward.

From there they set about the task of returning him to his former, ash-laden, statue-like appearance by applying a white, clay-like plant ooze that although a tad feminine for his taste, smelled far better than the drink he was just handed.

"What's this?" he said, making no effort to hide his displeasure. They giggled at his scrunched-up face.

"Kava," they told him. "It is Kava," motioning for him to drink up. "For you, yes?!"

"Kava," John repeated. "Mmmm," still smiling and nodding at everyone. "Smells like ass." They seemed pleased.

"Yes, ass, yes. You drink!" they mimicked. "Ass," they repeated to one another, smiling and nodding, pleased with their acquisition of this brand-new word.

Before he could politely turn them down, they pushed the coconut shell towards his face, causing him to take a huge, unwanted gulp.

Surprisingly, the taste was, in truth, tolerable. But the consistency... That was another matter. It had the consistency of tapioca. Tapioca, lumps, and all, that hadn't quite congealed. Throw in a few subtle notes of dirt, sulfur, and a hint of, I dunno...methane? (not to mention the lack of ice) and there you pretty much had a libation worthy as an offering to a deity.

Next, they wrapped him in a bark cloth sarong. "This will take a bit of getting used to," he muttered. Bark cloth was just that - a clothlike material made by battering the bark of the Mulberry tree until its fibers become pliable enough to fashion clothing out of it. Without the benefit of his comfy boxers running some interference, the "cloth" was a bit more abrasive on his nether region than he was used to. But it didn't seem to matter much. The little bit of Kava he'd taken was already providing the buzz equivalent of several shots of Patron and now, *all* his regions felt really, really good.

The women made their way to the village center leading John in his shiny new paint job towards the chanting and beating drums of a jungle party in full swing. He nervously wondered if this was their equivalent of a 4H fair and he was their blue-ribbon-hopeful prized pig. Once there, they seated him in an oversized chair carved out of a single Eucalyptus log and adorned him with various flowery accoutrements including a small headdress of sorts. The throne-like chair sat on the perimeter of a large, open air space that long ago had been stripped of its trees and shrubs leaving only a dusty, hard-packed, amber-colored clay circle where the villagers could gather to sing and dance just as their ancestors had done for centuries in times past. A firepit was its centerpiece and judging by the amount of combustible material in it, this was going to be one serious blaze.

"Always wanted to go to Burning Man," John thought to himself. As he looked about there were hundreds of villagers gyrating and pulsing in unison to the primitive rhythm generated by the log drummers. Every crazy form of dress imaginable - red, white, and blue, stars and stripes with brightly colored faces. The most unusual and out of place was the inordinate amount of foam stadium fingers worn prominently on the heads of most of the tribesmen. "Not too different," he thought, "than the Red Witch on Saturday night. Just wish I had a cold Corona. For that matter, a cold anything." But he didn't, so Kava was going to have to do. He held his breath and took another swig. He had to admit, as God - awful this stuff was it was all business and quickly getting the job done. Seated next to him was another masked villager, or so he thought, until he noticed a pricey video camera tucked away under a piece of brightly colored bark cloth.

"I'm John," he said.

"Marco," the man replied.

"Polo!" John quickly shot back. A confused look came across the man's face and John laughed out loud. "Not from the states? ...Never mind."

John noticed Marco's hand wrapped around a familiar coconut shell and smiled. He welcomed the idea of another westerner joining him in his journey down that long and winding Kava-filled trail that lay mysteriously ahead.

"Japan- I'm with the film crew? ...the documentary?" Marco smiled at him.

John hadn't heard. In fact, he hadn't heard much about anything since his crash. February 15th, the day of the annual Tanna Army USA parade, the day most of the islanders expect the return of John Frum had come and gone. What he was seeing was the remnants of that holiday, extraordinarily out-of-place, American-themed costumes and props were everywhere.

Marco was one of the fortunate few given rare permission by the council to stay beyond the date and visit the inner village. The few tourists who were allowed to witness the parade were always cordoned off on the beach and summarily dismissed back to their ship by day's end. The villagers' real, everyday utopian life was never put on display. Rather a watered-down version of what tourists expected to see was provided in exchange for a few fascinating trinkets brought ashore from the outside world.

John looked about. Dancing directly in front of them were a few of the men who were clearly beating them in the Kava consumption race, their eyes wild and threatening. Any fear, however, was put to rest by the broad smiles on their faces and the giant, neon-bright foam fingers with the inscription "WE'RE # 1" worn as hats on their heads.

"What's with the headgear?" John asked.

"That, my friend... is your latest cultural contribution to the village," Marco said, pausing only long enough to take another sip. John seemed confused. "Seems your chariot from the sky is leeching its magical cargo with every stiff breeze that comes along. Should have been here last week - raspberry ring pops and glow-in-the-dark rave necklaces," Marco said staring straight ahead. "And judging from that very fancy chair," pointing to John's hand-carved seat, "I think you just might be their guest of honor. Or their next meal." Marco laughed openly at his own joke. John chuckled nervously while sipping his drink. He held out his coconut shell, examining it.

"What's in this?" he asked.

"It's made from roots of the Kava plant," Marco explained, "more accurately, piper methysticum."

"Piper metha what? Can't be all bad if it starts with meth," John kidded him.

"Not quite the same...Several cultures use this in their rituals but this version of it? It's found nowhere else in the world." Marco was half contemplating, " Maybe it's because they actually chew the roots into paste balls and spit it into-"

"Oh my Ga... Whoa, whoa, whoa! Stop!" John pleaded. He physically shuddered, closing his eyes as to block out any and all remnants of that part of the conversation. Suddenly confused, John asked, "Then why do they drink it?"

"Because they can!" Marco was now laughing loudly.

"I mean, what's the significance in this whole ceremony thing- other than showing off their bad-ass hip hop skills?" A group of natives gyrated past them, "and their incredibly poor fashion sense."

"It was considered the devil's brew in the days of colonization. Missionaries hated it and tried to ban it," Marco said. "The locals believe it's a way to achieve Koontal."

"Koontal...what's that?" asked John.

"Loosely interpreted? Koontal. It means believing for the supernatural to occur in the physical realm. It's what enables them to sit out on that make-believe airfield night after night after night all these years. They think it'll bring about a quicker return of their Messiah," Marco explained.

"John Frum," added John.

"Ahhh very good! Yeah- so you know that when he returns... so does the stuff."

"Not exactly what you'd expect from such spiritual people," John quipped.

"At least it's honest," Marco pointed out. "The rest of the religious world disguises it by praying for "God's blessings"- Come'on!... that's code for stuff. Why not just pray, Dear God, please give me the 80" QLED Samsung and be done with it?"

"What type of stuff do you think they want?" John asked.

"Well, that's where they're just like us- they don't care- just stuff," a cynical Marco replied. "New stuff. Different stuff. Stuff stuff. When the allied forces first arrived, it introduced a poison into a pure, untainted society." He was now making his point loudly and emphatically. "It's because of that they'll never achieve Koontal!" No matter how much of this incredible Kava they drink!" he shouted. With that they "clinked" shells, spilling some. John laughed with his new friend and sat back, content to let Marco continue. "That's why a group of the elders retreated further into the interior. Separated themselves from the tainted ones. And the stuff. And the tourists. And.......this," motioning to the mild chaos about them. "Rumor has it they achieve Koontal all the time." A few of Marco's words had just a smidge of slur attached to them.

"There's others?" John asked. Marco paused and looked around. He took on that sudden drunk-seriousness and leaned in towards John.

"Yes," he said, nodding. "And they seem to be far more proficient in Koontal than the rest-without daily doses of this...." he squinted searching for the word, "liquid 'shrooms. I'm thinking it's some sort of genetic disposition at work here but there's no way to prove that. At least not from a senses man's perspective"

"Whoa, dude... English...." John implored him. "Census man or S. E. N. S. E. S. man?"

"Yeah. As in the five SENSES? Basically, all of mankind? If they can't see it, smell it, touch it, taste it, or hear it, it doesn't exist."

"Logical," John flatly stated.

"Precisely! Logic. Mankind's most useful tool that simultaneously blinds him to the profound realities of the sixth sense."

John whispers, "I see dead people." Marco looked confused. "Like ghosts, paranormal shit?" Marco quickly shook his head.

"Naaah, that's just one more distraction to get your eye off the prize."

An inebriated John falls into his best Tonto impression. "Hmmm, what exactly is prize, Kemosabe?"

"Believing."

"Believing" John parroted while nodding in mock seriousness. While a snickering John at this point had now been rendered incapable of being serious, the Kava had stripped what little humor Marco had left in him and he, on the other hand, was now dead serious and in full-blown pontification mode. Realizing the futility of trying to divert Marco's train of thought, John decided to simply sit back and for the sake of entertainment, watch it all go inevitably off the rails.

"Believing in its purest form - the absence of doubt. Believing for things to occur in your life as the need arises. Believing for things to occur that defy circumstances," each declaration accompanied by an emphatic finger-pointing and each becoming louder than the last. "The type of believing that pushes the boundaries of reality!" Marco suddenly went silent. He nodded, pointed with his eyes, drawing John's attention back to the circle. The crowd had parted leaving a solitary tribal member standing, facing them with his arms outstretched. No longer raising his voice, Marco finished his sentence.

"The type of believing that pushes the boundaries of reality... into the supernatural."

And with that, the tribesman stood, closed his eyes, and levitated himself a full 5 inches off the ground. John's mouth fell open.

"Parlor tricks," Marco stated flatly with mild disdain. Marco's attention turned back to John and once again leaned in, intent on driving his point home.

"This is believing that is impossible for most of us because of the self-imposed limitations of our belief in the five senses and LOGIC! How else do you explain a mother who is able to lift a fucking minivan off her pinned child by HERSELF!? WHAT IS THAT!?" John was dumbstruck. He stared at him, listening.

"It's impossible is what it is," Marco stated calmly. " Impossible. But it occurred. So how do you explain it?" He looked at John intently, skillfully waiting, letting it sink in. He reached out and rested his hand on his arm as John raised his drink for another sip.

"Before you take another drink, hear me out. This is important- you need to hear this. I mean really... need to hear this. What I found out was that in every single instance where this has occurred, there were two basic elements, two very specific requirements in evidence in order for this to happen." John's eyes were now glued to his. "Without them...?" he closed his eyes, "Poof."

"First, she had to believe it was possible. I mean, let's start there," he said. "Second, the circumstances had to have been so dire, so dire as to negate the possibility of doubt, and that's key. Because doubt is fear, and fear is believing in reverse- working contrary to the goal." Marco eyed John for a moment, gauging whether he was getting through." But when that happens, in that moment, in that very instant, is when we see the miraculous. It's when we witness the truly.... supernatural."

It was all a bit much for John. He wasn't sure if the effects of the Piper Methawhatever had made him hallucinate or did this all just happen? What was most perplexing was that Marco spoke a truth that he had never heard before but somehow always knew. It was meeting someone for the first time after viewing their Facebook pictures for years. John didn't know it at the time, but this was one of the most important conversations of his life. If what Marco had said was true, it meant that anything was possible. Anything. Without exception and that impossibility, itself ceased to exist. John suddenly snapped out of his Kava-induced, blank stare haze.

"So, how'd you learn about this?"

"I found a treasure map I guess," Marco replied. John smiled thinking his leg was being pulled.

"Where'd you find that?" he asked with a smirk. Marco laughed and shook his head.

"Ya' know, leave something in plain sight and nobody finds it." He took another long drink. "I mean it's only been there for a couple of thousand years."

"So why are they hiding out in the jungle?" John asked.

"They may look like primitives, but they're smart enough to realize there are some in the world who see that kind of power as an incredible threat. And, well... it is!"

"Geez! You sound just like a friend of mine." You don't happen to know-"

John's inquiry was cut short by the sudden shift in Marco's expression. He was looking to his left at a group of tribesmen. They were larger than the rest and although appropriately costumed, seemed somehow out of place. They stood silently, their eyes cast in John and Marco's direction.

"What's that all about?" John asked. Marco cleared his throat.

"Perhaps I've allowed the Kava to influence my better judgment. Let me leave you with this."

He proceeded to scribble a cryptic note and stuffed it into one of the folds of John's bark cloth sarong. Marco abruptly raised himself and walked towards the jungle path leading away from the village center. The men followed. Directly behind them was another. His mask was pushed to one side. He glanced back at John. John was taken aback. It was Professor Wharton and, in his hand, came the glint of a long blade. Or so it appeared. At the same time, as if on cue, the dancing throng surrounded John effectively creating a human curtain, blocking his view. Any hope of confirming his Wharton sighting was lost. Did he really just see Professor Wharton, his business professor following someone into the dark and foreboding jungle like a common thug or was the Kava just playing with his mind? It couldn't be, could it?

Regardless, he had no time to consider it. His view was increasingly more of the same- sweaty, wild-eyed villagers dancing far too close to him and the numerous torches. Drunk or not he did have the presence of mind to realize he didn't want to be this close while wearing a bark sarong when the inevitable happened. He placed his hands together and then pulled them apart, fanning his fingers in a symbolic gesture of parting the crowd. "Just like the Red Sea," he muttered. "Let my people go!" he shouted in his best Charlton Heston voice.

Miraculously they began to do just that. The drums grew louder and louder and in a final, deafening crescendo suddenly stopped. There, standing in the gap was the silhouette of a woman of untold beauty. Dressed in a form-fitted, feathery costume, her bronze, polished skin shone against the pure white feathers that were strategically placed on her body. Her large, almond-shaped, emerald-green eyes stood in stark contrast against the sea of brown eyes normally found throughout the region. She stood silently, her legs parted slightly, her arms hanging loosely by her side, her eyes locked with John's.

The drums began again. Slowly at first but with an ever-increasing cadence as she began her dance. As she slowly made her way forward, one by one the men would run out to her, fall to their knees in the dust and with arms outstretched, offer themselves to be taken by her. She in turn would face them dancing seductively and one by one ultimately reject them by pushing them over with her well-defined, extended leg. The men would laugh with each rejection as the music grew louder, faster.

John was impossibly mesmerized by her. The closer she got the more he wished he hadn't allowed himself to get so wasted. And that he was. By the time she was close enough for him to really see her, it was difficult to tell what was real and what was not. But things went from bad to worse. His worst nightmare had just come true. The woman that had cared for him, the beautiful, compassionate face of his coma-induced visions, the girl of his dreams was now standing before him and he was so shit-faced he could barely speak.

The jungle vixen pushed over the last rejected suitor and turned her body towards John, locking her eyes with his. The intricate tribal face paint was both scary and seductive but there was no mistaking her eyes. The urgency in the ever-increasing chants, the pulsing rhythm of the drums became hypnotic, and her body was responding, her eyes closed in wanton abandon.

She reached up and plucked the most prominent white feather from her headdress and grasping it between her fingers, placed it in the same fold Marco had placed the mysterious note. Without missing a beat, she had palmed the note and tracing a line with her hand down her cleavage made it disappear.

She was now so close several drops of her flowery scented perspiration fell onto his ash white face. She reached out and wiped his face as she had every day after his crash. John was captivated and sat staring longingly at her. Running through his head was one thought and one thought only.

"Oh God!" he thought, "Don't puke."

Too late.

CHAPTER 10

TIME FOR A
MYSTERIOUS VISIT

John woke to Sam's face mere inches away from his and sniffing him. Again.

"Geez! Dude! I HATE when you do that! Ooooh, my head!" John cradled his head with his hands. Sam was grinning ear to ear and offered him more Kava. "Ugh! Oooh, no thanks, no." John noticed a crude, hand-carved medallion hanging from Sam's neck. It was of a nautilus shell, a cutaway version of it, and John reached to examine it. Sam quickly recoiled and looked at him suspiciously, his smile erased.

"Oh, sorry! I saw that last night. On that girl. That incredible, hot, unbelievably sexy girl. The way she moved her assaaaaay!! Good mornin' little sunshine!" John abruptly stopped. He hadn't noticed 10-year-old Heylia who had been standing behind Sam listening to his every word, smiling and wide-eyed. John sheepishly smiled at her.

"Hungry you?" She said as she began pulling out some freshly baked breadfruit fries out of her basket.

"We walk you eat, yes?" Sam insisted.

John quickly pulled himself together all the while thinking he'd give a king's ransom for a double latte right now. He politely accepted the little girls' offering and munched on them as they headed away from the village.

"They're good, Heylia," John said, nodding his approval.

Sam led him to the airfield. They wound their way up a steep mountainous trail to the top of a long ridge where years ago the villagers had carved out a replica of the hastily made WWII airstrip. It was primitive to say the least and if it was once plane-worthy, it certainly wasn't now. There were deep ruts and rivulets in the dirt strip from the daily torrential rains and should any plane have made the mistake of actually trying to land there, it would have been destroyed within seconds of touchdown. At the south end of the field there was a three-story tower constructed entirely of bamboo and manned with a villager who continued to scan the skies through his make-believe bamboo binoculars. Leaning against the tower a flagman stood at the ready in the only strip of shade on the entire mountaintop with flags made from someone's cast away Lynyrd Skynyrd T-shirt. Another slept across the hood of a bamboo Jeep that was parked just off the airstrip. A plane sat at the north end of the field, it too made entirely of bamboo and poised for takeoff. They were surprisingly good representations of the real thing.

"Kite koe? He rite hoki koutou hoki matou," Sam excitedly stated. Heylia stepped in to interpret.

"You see? We are ready for the return. Our ancestors in sky will guide here."

John began to understand. They were seeking his approval. By now John had given up trying to convince them that he was NOT John Frum and found it best to simply guide the conversation down a different path.

"I understand you've been here a long time Sam," John said.

"Yes. Yes. Long time. Every night we come, we stay, watch heavens. Sometimes very dangerous."

"How so?" John asked.

"Giants come. Ghosts. Ghost giants. Take our women and disappear into air. Some very 'fraid but they still come," he said.

"They disappear? How?" John asked.

Rather than explaining, Sam pantomimed, drawing his hands back and making a sucking sound. He acted as if he'd been thrown to the ground on his back. It was all too familiar to John, but this far away, and here?

"Are you afraid Sam?"

Sam smiled and shook his head no. "I use torch." Sam lunged forward as one would in a fencing match, stabbing with his lance. "They no like fire," he said laughing.

"So how does this whole Koontal thing work?"

"For me?" Sam asked.

"Sure, ok."

"Little bit Kava. Not lot. Little. Lot make you huarangi," Sam searched for the word ".... crazy. You born with Koontal. You no need Kava."

"I don't know about that," an unconvinced John said.

Sam walked over to the nearest tree and stripped a switch from it. He found a heavier branch on the ground that formed a Y and handed it to John. He positioned the switch between the two legs of the Y and began tapping each leg.

"No can think two thinks at one time," he said. "No can do." Tapping back and forth between the branch's legs, he would say the word, "Think. Think. Think. Think," with each tap. Sam began to slap each branch very quickly. "Very fast...but no two thinks at same time!"

It struck John that Sam's point was identical to one Professor Wharton had spoken of years ago in one of his first classes.

"People think they can think two things at once— if you ask them, they'll swear to it," he'd say, but in reality, they're merely toggling between two thoughts at a high rate of speed. Thinking two thoughts at precisely the same time is as impossible as two forms of matter occupying the same space at the same time."

Sam stopped and pointed to the left branch.

"This Koontal...believe." Pointing to the right branch, "This Rangirua... uhh..." Sam looked to his granddaughter searching for the word.

"Feaa," she said, "ummm... doubt!"

"Yes!" Sam proclaimed, "Doubt! Doubt! This doubt," pointing to the right branch leg. He took the Y branch from John and gave him the switch. "Now you do." John slapped the branches using a windshield wiper motion. Sam inserted his hand, preventing the switch from striking the right branch of doubt. "My hand...is little bit of Kava," Sam continued eyeing John. He then removed it and John stopped.

"No stop! Faster!" Sam shouted, startling John into continuing. John was now breaking a sweat as he tried to go even faster still. Suddenly, almost violently, Sam reached out and grabbed the switch as it struck the left branch of Koontal, the branch of believing, and held it fast against it. He looked at John intensely and uncomfortably long. John wondered, had he done something wrong? Slowly a smile began to form on Sam's face. He was slowly nodding, like a caring teacher watching a new discovery dawn on his pupil.

"You choose your thinks, John Frum. You choose believe - no doubt. You, John Frum... no need Kava." Extending his long, weathered finger, Sam tapped on John's forehead. "Your Kava here."

"It is time, John Frum," bellowed a voice from behind.

John turned to see who was addressing him. His eyes met with a group of villagers dressed from head to toe in their ceremonial garb. By now he was more or less accustomed to being confronted with the most bizarre items of clothing and decoration. Chicken's feet necklaces were particularly popular as were porcupine quill hats, but this group had a whole new slant. These fashion-forward Beau Brummel's had all chosen to share a similar theme this time- a combination of vintage army surplus with Euro rave party necklaces and ring pops. And plenty of them. John couldn't help but feel a tad responsible this new trend, that he, or more accurately his spilled cargo might have been the source of their inspiration. One poor soul had so many glow-in-the-dark necklaces strung about his neck that his eyes were barely visible. But beneath it, John could make out a familiar shape just hanging around his neck.

"Jesus! Is that a real mortar round!?" John stepped back in disbelief.

"Silence!" the group's leader demanded.

Wordlessly he motioned to the men who then proceeded to grab each of John's arms and led him to a large rock. It wasn't threatening, no one ever really seemed genuinely threatening. They just never bothered with formalities. Like asking if grabbing you was ok. It was efficient in getting things done to say the least- for them.

The rock was covered in spattered remnants of washed-out white paint. At least that's what John hoped it was. Earlier he had seen a large number of Nazca Boobies, a name that stuck with him and every other giggling, pubescent fifth grader, and their droppings were particularly pungent. He wasn't keen on the idea of laying himself down in that. They stripped him naked and began to pelt him with the white ash, covering him from head to toe. "What is up with this constant white-washing!?" he wondered. "Was this the official uniform of an ever-mistaken messiah?" he thought.

"Mutu!" yelled the group's leader.

The men immediately stopped and backed away, allowing the shop foreman to critique their work. John was hacking like an aging, Pennsylvania coal miner while trying to clear the ash from his eyes. Apparently satisfied with John's new look, the leader reached into a canvas gunny sack and began removing some of John's things. Among them, his cargo pants he'd been wearing on the day he "dropped in", his boots and more importantly, his magic box cell phone. He quickly put them on and placed the cell phone in one of the pockets. One of the men approached him with eyes lowered and arms outstretched holding a coconut shell filled with Kava. He motioned for John to take it. Luckily for John, there was much more shell than there was liquid but now resigned, John raised his shell to the crowd, muttered "cheers" and tossed it back like a shot of cheap tequila at a Super Bowl party.

"Ughhh," he shuddered.

They brought out a bright red chair with wide armrests adorned with the skulls of what looked like wild boar and draped in the skins they used to live in. John had become rather good at interpreting their actions and without prompting, walked over towards the chair, and sat in it. Only later would he find out that by sitting in it he had accepted the challenge and all that went with it. Without warning, two poles appeared and slid through the rings beneath the armrest. He was suddenly raised and being run down a dirt path deep into the jungle and away from the airfield. John looked back, quickly scanning the crowd, and caught a last glimpse of Sam's face as he bounced down the path. Sam, forever smiling, was still doing that, which gave John some much-needed assurance that things would be ok, whatever they had planned. He really didn't know Sam all that well, but John had always lived by the saying *judge a tree by the fruit that it bears*" and well, Sam so far had produced some truly wholesome fruit. There was a kindness about him, an honesty that despite the language barrier, despite the cultural divide that told John that Sam was a man who could be trusted.

After a good forty-five minutes of jostling and untold numbers of Bislamic campfire singing chants, they arrived at a small clearing. The ground was covered in a thick carpet of soft, green moss and the light coming from the treetops came down in perfect Broadway theater pin spots. Directly in the center of the light was something so out of place, so bizarre that for the first few moments it refused to compute in John's brain. Deep in the heart of this remote island's jungle, in the middle of absolutely nowhere was Stonehenge. It was smaller, but a perfectly scaled Stonehenge. At first, he started to question the men but quickly realized that they would have no answers. Gauging by their reverence, this was one of their holiest of places in their culture and as far as they were concerned, had no beginning, and had no end.

"This must be the place Marco was talking about - the interior," he thought. The place where those who had seriously developed their skills, the elders, had come he surmised. There certainly had been very few visitors to this spot over the centuries. For some reason, his feelings led him to believe that perhaps this pathway would lead to a place where answers about his own life could be found as well.

There appeared to be an entrance gate to the circle. Two large grey stones placed as columns on either side bridged with a massive headstone. A hieroglyphic-like inscription across the top had been all but worn away except for one figure in particular whose head was disproportionately larger than his body and he was being pushed against by a large group of much smaller figures. The fact that it had remained visible when all the others had worn away, told him that in all likelihood, it had been chiseled in sometime later and was probably a record of a more recent history. "Was this a record of Sam's Ghost giants?" he wondered.

The men had John stand with his back to the entrance gate. There was a moment of complete silence from the group and then an odd, mechanical hissing noise overwhelmed the area. It took him a moment to figure out that it was in truth coming from the villagers themselves but like well-trained ventriloquists, no one's lips moved. Suddenly three men appeared from behind him. John presumed the three were the so-called elders. The only explanation was they somehow simply materialized as John had just looked at the stone circle and there had been no one there but now, they stood before him.

John's confused look prompted one of the elders to step forward and speak to him.

"Haere ki nga roto!"

He stepped back to allow a second elder to come forward.

"Haere ki nga roto!"

and then followed by a third,

"Haere ki nga roto!"

John had no idea what was being said but something about it was oddly familiar. The timing, the rhythm of the words.... he had heard it somewhere before. Then it dawned on him. John smiled in realization, shook his head and muttered,

"Surrender Dorothy!"

He was now approached by the group's leader who had apparently gotten the lion's share of the ring pops and rave necklaces. Unlike the others, however, he chose to wear his stadium foam finger not as a hat, but rather as a sheath covering his genitals. As he walked towards John drenched in his bling, his neon-green foam finger began to create its own rhythmic, side to side motion as it pointed the way forward.

John's head dropped in what he hoped would be perceived as an act of reverence, but fact be known, it was a desperate move to hide his disbelief and laughter. As he did, they placed a necklace of glow sticks around his neck, none of which had been activated.

"What, no ruby red slippers?" he thought.

The remaining villagers stepped back ceremoniously. Lord Fingerdick stood before him and with his blackened, almost toothless grin spreading across his face, he inserted one of the many red ring pops into his mouth. First twisting and turning it, he pulled it out with a pop causing John to laugh. It was quickly apparent that this part of the ceremony was deadly serious, and he had just come dangerously close to insulting them. As he extended the ring pop out towards John, a long suspension bridge of spittle followed it, hanging from it like a tired bungee cord. The sudden puzzled look on the leader's face at John's hesitation told him that he was to accept this treasured gift and he made every effort to do so without touching the wet part. His reluctance was interpreted as ungratefulness and did not go unnoticed as each villager began coaching him through elaborate hand gestures. He was to share it by putting it into his own mouth and between the two of them, over time, whittle it down to nothing. John's hesitation was not received well. The hissing noise that had continued throughout suddenly stopped. The smiles were gone and for the first time, it felt a bit menacing. Almost as a reflex, John placed both of his hands piously together, bowing as he slowly backed away.

"Namaste'... namaste."

Cliche as it was, John beat his chest as he had seen in a classic Tarzan movie, crushing the capsules within the glow sticks. Suddenly his face was awash with a bright, neon-green glow, making him appear a bit menacing himself. Time to show his perfect pearly whites he thought having read somewhere that in the animal kingdom that was interpreted as aggression.

As the villagers watched in a renewed sense of awe, John made one more final step back, placing him between the stone columns and directly beneath the gate's imposing headstone. There was a tremendous sucking sound and in an instant, he was gone. Several of the elders, knocked down from the force emanating from the gate's opening and closing, simply stared at the gate. No one seemed shocked, all in a day's work it seemed. The group began to settle in, preparing themselves for what would most certainly be a long wait.

Just as quickly as he entered, he exited, only miles away, close to the coast. The topography was vastly different and the smells and sounds of the ocean were apparent. No longer the sometimes claustrophobic greenery blotting out the sun, the oppressive dank of jungle humidity quickly sapping his strength and energy. Instead a wide open, sun drenched panorama greeted him with cool, fresh breezes that carried the refreshing smell of freedom and escape. Stepping out from a natural stone outcropping, he stumbled towards the sound of breaking surf. He was dazed, like someone thrown from a horrific car crash, wandering about without purpose. Covering his face he wore a two-week-old stubble and much of his ash white paint job had worn off and was scuffed and dirty. Hanging about his neck from a thin leather strap was a tiny leather satchel filled with miniature nautilus shells of every color. When he finally made the clearing, he found himself on a large rock-strewn beach. There in front of him stood four men. Three native elders and one white man. He called out for help but found his voice all but gone. The man raced forward to help him and John collapsed in his arms. He pulled his head back trying to focus on his rescuer's face. "Can't be!" he thought. "Wharton?"

"Don't speak," he quickly said.

The elders stepped up, addressing the professor.

"Kua whakaturia tona aroaro te karaka i roto i te motini."

"(His presence has set the clock in motion)."

"hoki te aha"

("For what?") asked Professor Wharton.

"Te hokinga nui ... kohikohi nga Repaima i te kuwaha. Me ia faaineine ia koe."

"(The great return... The giants gather at the gate. You must prepare him)."

"Ka tatou karanga a ka haere mai koutou?"

"(We shall call, and you shall come?)" the elder asked.

"E tatou."

"(We will)," affirmed the professor.

"Hohoro te haere, te whai ratou!"

"(Go quickly, one follows!)" Professor Wharton shook his head.

"Man, if this isn't Deja Vu all over again."

The three elders backed into the rocks and trees and in some *Harry & the Hendersons* camouflage moment, were swallowed into the background leaving no footprints. Unbeknownst to the pair, the "one" following was much closer than they had realized. But this was no ordinary guy. He moved with incredible speed through the thick underbrush and soon the sound of snapping branches could be heard. As he drew ever closer, the now frantic thrashing was mixed with exaggerated, heavy breathing and punctuated with scary, animal-like grunts and snarls. Whoever or whatever this was, was clearly not racing towards them for a last-minute hug. Whatever its intentions, John and the professor had no intention of hanging around to find out. Wasting no time, Professor Wharton straightened John up, slung his arm across his own shoulders and began to push him towards the water's edge where he had hidden a small skiff behind one of the barnacle-encrusted boulders. It was low tide, so the small boat was now perched on the sand. The professor tried getting John to lend a hand in dragging the boat to the retreating sea, but John was still in some post-trauma haze and was of little help. Still dazed and somewhat oblivious, he stopped and looked over at the professor.

"Wharton?"

Right now, John was that annoying, drunk friend who stops in the middle of a busy street to light a cigarette.

"Come with me if you want to live," the professor said.

"Come vith me if you vant to live," John mimicked in his better than average Arnold Schwarzenegger impression. *"Terminator,"* Arnol-"

Professor Wharton grabbed John by the arm before he could finish and began dragging him into the boat.

"Hey!" John protested loudly as Professor Wharton tried his first pull on the engine's starter cord. With each subsequent pull the professor spoke to John,

"You FAIL to GRASP the GRAVITY of our SITUATION... HERE!"

And with that final pull, the engine roared to life. He lost no time speeding away from the beach, heading straight out to sea. He looked back towards the shoreline just in time to see a disturbance in the coconut palms and then a virtual explosion of jungle debris as their pursuer broke the tree line. Professor Wharton's heart sank.

"A Neph," he muttered. "Shit. Sure hope he hasn't learned to swim over the last thirty years."

John was slumped in the back, his eyes at half-mast staring straight ahead towards a choppy horizon. Professor Wharton, piloting the less than adequately powered skiff, continued to glance back over his shoulder trying to keep one eye on the threat and the other on a disappearing sun. But the Neph had seemingly disappeared and hopefully given up the pursuit allowing him his first chance to breathe a sigh of relief. It was short-lived. The Neph's head broke the surface only ten feet behind them, gulping in air and then disappearing below the churning wake. They both looked at each other in horror and sheer disbelief. Surely it couldn't keep swimming- they were already nearly five hundred yards offshore!

"We're gonna need a bigger boat," Professor Wharton said.

In an effort of futility, he thrust the throttle forward, but it was already as far as it would go. Its gargantuan head broke the surface again briefly and disappeared once more. Suddenly a giant hand appeared on the stern. It was human, only twice the size it should have been, its knuckles gnarled and grotesque looking. The boat slowed noticeably as this new, monstrous weight latched on. Without thinking, John grabbed the nearest weapon, the stern anchor, and swung it down on the beast's hand. His first panicked attempt missed, knocking a hole in the bottom of the boat the size of a small grapefruit. This time rather than swinging it, he picked the anchor up and slammed it down directly on to its hand causing him to let go. Water was now pouring into the skiff and John frantically searched for something to begin bailing with. At the same time, the Neph's head popped out of the water and was gulping air with a low, throaty gurgling noise. His long black hair covered most of his bearded face but what was most notable was the sheer size of it. He took a swing at the back of the boat attempting to latch on once again but came up short. Instead, he managed to knock the outboard engine up, taking the propeller out of the water. The sudden release from the water's resistance at full speed caused the propeller to completely shear off, leaving only the propeller's shaft spinning and whining like a gigantic dentist's

TIME FOR A MYSTERIOUS VISIT

drill. They were effectively dead in the water and if something didn't change, and soon, *they* would quite literally be dead in the water.

John, now wide awake and alert, was frantically bailing while Professor Wharton worked at shutting down the motor to stop that deafening, God-awful screaming engine noise. The boat began to tip backward as the seawater poured in.

" Anytime you wanna shut that thing down will be fine with me!" John sarcastically shouted above the whine.

"It's off!" Professor Wharton shouted back.

"Then what in hell is that noi-"

Suddenly the sun was blotted out in shadow and they were deluged in a wall of sea water that washed them over the side and into the churning surf. When they surfaced, the water surrounding them had turned bright red. Immediately Professor Wharton began frantically calling John's name.

"John! Are you alright? Are you hurt, what is this, are you bleeding!?"

"I'm fine, are you!?" answered John.

"I'm alright."

John felt something big touch his back- the universal nightmare of anyone who has swum in the ocean. He let out a startled scream but sucked in a lungful of seawater instead. As he choked and coughed, he instinctively swam away from whatever it was, frantically peering around him trying to see what it was lurking in the water. He turned around and a dark shadow just below the surface now rose, floating to the top. It was a human body, quite dead as it was missing its head. But as he reached the professor who was now clinging to the overturned skiff, he looked back at it once again and saw that it was no ordinary human. It was nearly twice the normal size with large garish features, it's joints overly pronounced and a good deal hairier than most.

John looked at Professor Wharton shaking his head signaling his unspoken message, "WTF?"

From the other side of the boat came a voice.

"Ugghh! ...Manky! Bugger sure does bleed a lot." The silver fuselage of a Boeing 314 Clipper floated into view. "Get in!"

It was Aiden. He had swooped down and in one precise maneuver used the landing pontoon as a knife blade, removing the Neph's grotesque head. Certainly out of place, considering the harrowing circumstances, John and the professor burst into laughter of relief and swam towards the waiting pontoon.

CHAPTER 11

LUCY, YOU GOT SOME SPLAININ' TO DO

M*eanwhile, back home...*
Just off a little used walking trail along a small, hidden pond sat Professor Wharton and his dog, Jack. Jack, a sweetheart of a dog but you'd never know it by looking at him. He was a Mastiff/Pitbull mix who had what felt like two boneless chicken breasts under his sleek fur on his forehead, muscles that were dedicated entirely to creating bone crushing bite pressure. When he'd yawn and it was like looking down the throat of a hippopotamus, only with sharper teeth. He'd spent the first eighteen months of his life training to be a prize fighter until Social Services raided his owners' home and placed him in a local shelter. The professor often brought him to class to socialize him, although he spent most of his time napping under his desk. Most students loved him. Others were scared to death.

Jack's head popped up as John approached, then realizing it was only John, put his head back down to continue his sun-drenched nap. A fishing pole sat between two rocks and an idle float drifted a couple of feet out on the surface of the water. A metallic green tackle box supported Professor Wharton's feet on top of a beat-up cooler filled with a few beers and a sandwich. Professor Wharton continued staring off towards the far shore of the pond.

"The ones on the bottom are cold," he said, motioning towards the cooler. John reached in, rummaged around, and popped the top on the coldest one he could find.

"Thanks. I gotta tell ya', I am just this side of a little freaked out."

"Business Marketing 101?" said the professor, looking him dead in the eye. A lone eyebrow raised, and his head lowered ever so slightly. "It just isn't that hard and with a few of these tutoring sessions, you'll get it- don't worry."

He casually held a finger to his lips. John had never noticed the nautilus tattoo on the professor's forearm before or the nautilus ring on his finger for that matter. He had lived his entire life without ever giving them a thought and suddenly nautiluses were everywhere.

"Jack!" whispered Professor Wharton. He removed the nautilus ring from his finger and attached it to his collar.

"Jack! Ale'!" he snapped, and Jack turned lumbering away down the forest trail. He turned to John and motioned for him to follow in silence.

Professor Wharton led him back into the woods and into a small clearing filled with magnolia trees. They were more bushes than trees really but did an excellent job of hiding the entrance to a long-forgotten salt mine. Right from the start the shaft went perilously downward and within 50 feet seemed to end in a small pool filled with rainwater and woodsy debris. But as John would find out, just before the pool began, the darkness hid an old, padlocked doorway hidden from view by a small rock ledge protruding out from the left. The professor opened the door and flipped on the light.

"Batteries," he said to a confused John. "It's ok," he continued. "You're not walking into the next episode of *Dexter*." John smiled nervously.

" What *is* all this shit?" John asked.

"Stuff," Professor Wharton corrected him.

"Stuff," John replied.

"Old, abandoned salt mine. Three more feet?... they might've discovered these humongous veins of copper. Welcome to nature's perfect Faraday cage." John looked baffled. "Yeah, not what you'd expect in the middle of the woods. I guess you can tell it's been here a while," he said while brushing away the cobwebs.

"How'd you-"

"Look, I know you've got a million questions, but we only have a little while before Jack comes back... and when he does, we'll be back on their radar so-"

"Whose radar? And what's with the ring?"

"OK! Zip it. Take a seat John. Take a seat!!" the professor insisted.

"So, you worked with my father?" Professor Wharton just smiled knowingly.

"I guess you've noticed how you're able to do things... amazing things sometimes?"

"Not really," John said matter of factly. Professor Wharton rolled his eyes.

"This is gonna be harder than I thought. Yes, you can and yes you do." John was slouching. "Sit up straight. OK, that big guy coming at us from the jungle? They're called Nephilim. They used to rule the world way back when until God stepped in and wiped them out with the great flood."

"God?" John, smirking, couldn't resist pointing out the irony of this coming from his Darwinian fan boy teacher.

"Except He didn't quite finish the job. They now co-exist with us but on a different plane, a different dimension. Normally we never see them."

"Then what I saw outside the bar was one of them. I was at this-"

"Yeah, I know," he interrupted. John was surprised at that. "One of the good watchers," the professor continued. "They normally don't appear just anywhere- they're restricted to certain portals and certain times- Bermuda triangle, the pyramids. This is new and that's what's troubling."

"Good Watchers. Presumably then there are bad watchers?"

"Yeah. Doesn't make sense that you'd sell out your own race but power or even the *hope* of power can be compelling. Fletcher Howard. Remember that name- he's the worst of them. He's the reason why Sam walks the way he does."

"Sam? Gentle Sam?

"Yeah, and countless others. He's the one that rounded everybody up including your mother. Somebody's dictating what he does and when he does it but he's the muscle."

"What do they want with Tanna?" John asked.

"The tree. One stinkin' tree, the source of the tupu harore. The single ingredient in Kava that temporarily blocks the brain's ability to doubt. You have a little experience in knowing what's possible when doubt is eliminated." John's eyebrows raised. "Your recent crossing

Hamilton Street to get to the quiz... to name just one? Anyway, they get that they control the Nephs."

"Do you know where it is?" asked John.

"Never did. Until you landed smack dab on top of it," Professor Wharton laughed. "What are the odds? Regardless, Fletcher must never find out."

"Seriously....How'd you know exactly where I'd pop out of that twilight zone anyway?" There was a long, contemplative pause. Professor Wharton looked away and then back at John.

"Because that's where your father came out 24 years ago." John sprang out of his seat.

"Wait! He's been there!?"

"Yeah. But he wasn't lucky enough to have someone on the outside waiting to show him the way home. Fletcher and the watchers were there instead. And once they saw he made it through... well, they made his life a living hell. So far, you've managed to stay out of their line of sight-except for that little...trying to kill you thing. That's why we're here. It's time you realize who you are and what's at stake."

John's voice lowered, "Is he still alive?"

"Very much so."

"And my mother?"

"I'll talk. You listen." Professor Wharton dusted off a chair and motioned for John to sit down.

"30 years ago, a crib sat empty in a field office smack dab in the middle of one of the densest jungles in the South Pacific archipelago. Your mother set it up as a reminder to your father that you were very much part of the plan." They both smiled. "Your parents were botanists and part of a team sent by the government to study why these indigenous people seemed to possess...special abilities. There was a lot of weird stuff happening while the Americans occupied the island and certain people took notice. Hitler had his clairvoyant's and the Americans wanted to balance the scales with the Elders. The Japanese were certainly interested as well."

"Koontal," John quickly added. Professor Wharton began laughing.

"Ahhh, so you *do* remember your little conversation with Marco! Yes, Koontal."

"Is he alright? That guy who carted him away..."

"Oh, he's fine. Can't say as much for his escort..."

"Are you some sort of badass that we don't know about?" John asked. The professor chose to ignore his question.

"Anyway, it wasn't too long before we discovered the government's interest was far from scientific- it was military or some such. At that point we decided to slow the process down without being obvious and learn all that we could hoping we could develop the skills ourselves- and somehow prevent it from becoming just another weapon in their arsenal."

"Were you able to pull that off?" asked John.

"Your father was. He was a lot like you." The professor took a pensive, long held blink. "It's not that he was anything special, no offense. It's like being born with.... perfect teeth. It's not an accomplishment. It just happens. What's different is that he recognized it, developed it."

"And he was able to keep it hidden?"

"For a while. But when they did get an idea that we had made a bit more progress than we were letting on, they sent in some observers. Your uncle for one. Your uncle started out a decent guy, but he unwittingly made a huge error. He called in for supplies and had 'em airlifted in."

"Geez," John rolled his eyes and shook his head.

"You see where this is going. The tribe's been watching your father's steady improvement in Koontal and is already wondering if he's the long-awaited Messiah. Well, when that sky filled up with parachutes it was a done deal. They whisked him off to the interior for the elders to check him out. Sound familiar?"

"And that's when he popped out and these "watchers" grabbed him. So as far as the villagers were concerned, he just never came back? Is that when they interrogated him?" John's question prompted the professor's confused, wary look.

"Yeah. How'd you know that?"

"Aiden. On the flight over."

"That stupid son of bi-"

"Whoa, whoa, whoa! It's my fault. I used my persuasive superpowers and pried it out of him," John said through a sarcastic smile.

"Would have been just as easy to have offered him a shot of Jack Daniels wearing a push-up bra."

"Is it true? I mean the whole story?"

"Yeah. Yeah, that's how your uncle became your uncle." Professor Wharton's face indicated he had just had a thought. "I'm wondering.... whether he took his chip out after all these years. I just assumed but never asked..."

"What, like a rescue dog?" John asked.

"See this tattoo? Hides the scar where I took mine out soon after I got it. A paring knife at the kitchen table-"

"Ughh!" John shuddered.

"If you don't get it out, eventually it'll actually change your DNA. Turn 'ya hybrid. Put mine in that fine ring I wear. As far as they're concerned, we're up at the cabin enjoying a few more cold ones. I'm gonna give you an anti-bugging app on your phone. Your uncle's been acting kinda funny of late-Let's see if he's still chipped."

He grabbed John's phone and walked over to the workbench. John began to walk about, rummaging through the billion or so oddities scattered throughout the room. The mind-boggling mixture of high-tech, low tech, old tech pieces of equipment were hard to take in. He could have spent an entire week using the same phrase- "What's this for?" John was fascinated.

"So, is there some significance to this nautilus thing?" John asked while holding an old RCA vacuum tube up to the light for closer inspection.

"Yeah. It's symbolic. It's symbolic of the concentration of believing-Don't touch that- as well as a way of identifying the true believers." Professor Wharton suddenly raised his head, listening. A distant bark from Jack was heard. "Crap. What's he doing back here? Here take this," the professor said as he kicked a dusty, wooden crate towards him.

"What's this?" John asked. "It's heavy."

"It's everything your father saw while in the interior and probably what you saw too. With any luck, it'll jog your memory... maybe answer some of the questions you have." He wrote an address on the box.

"Go to this location, see the curator there-he's a friend of mine-and ask for Em."

John was confused. "M? Just M? Where am I going, MI6?"

"Emerald," Professor Wharton said, "Her name is Emerald."

"What's there?" asked John.

"Answers."

John grabbed the crate and turned to go.

"And Nephilim," the professor added. John stopped dead in his tracks and slowly turned back towards him. "Oh, don't worry- these are dead. Been dead for quite some time. And John? Be careful. Never know who you can trust."

John smiled. "I'm still lookin' at you."

Professor Wharton smiled back. "You're smarter than you look."

It was dusk when John turned the latch on his apartment house door. Ever since the 'incident at the Red Witch', as it became known, he took to checking his surroundings more than usual and always stopped and listened before entering- even in his own apartment. His concern certainly wasn't theft- after all, it was a typical college apartment where most of what little furniture there was, was made of pallet wood and painted cinder blocks.

There were numerous boxes lining the hallway floor, filled with trophies and achievement plaques all left unhung and not displayed, a testament to his lack of interest in them. Interestingly, it was a select few primitive pieces that made the cut and were on display- a foreshadowing of his future path, perhaps. Other than a framed vintage movie poster of Peter Sellers' "Being There", it was pretty much nothing but off-white walls wherever you looked.

John opened the fridge and stared into the empty, white void. The bare bulb revealed the same inventory as when he had left. Nothing but a large, filtered water pitcher, an open pack of string cheese, a to-go carton with God-only-knows-what inside, a single craft beer and three different types of hot sauce. He grabbed the lone beer, wiped the top with his shirt and using the hinge on the cabinet door, popped it open and began sifting through the mountain of papers inside Wharton's mystery crate.

Much of it looked like typed up lab notes- handwritten chemical symbols scribbled in the margins complete with scratched out sections, nothing compelling to say the least. But in one folder, amidst the notes was a black and white photograph. It was the same photograph as the one that fell into his lap in the cockpit of Miss Edna. But unlike that one, this one wasn't missing the bottom right-hand corner. There was a little girl, no more than 4 or 5 dressed in her village finery, grinning from ear to ear, her big, bright eyes staring straight into the camera's lens. John turned it over and in pencil, the names of each had been written. All but the little girl's. It had been erased causing John to wonder who she was and why her name had been removed.

It had served to cause John to now go through each stack of documents more carefully, more methodically. When he finally reached the bottom of the crate, it was nearly 1am and without all the papers covering the crate's wooden interior the musty smell of years of mildew filled the room. There was one last photograph, but its corner had gotten stuck in a crack of the wooden bottom. John gently tugged on it and when he did, he noticed the entire bottom moved. "A false bottom!" he said to himself. He rummaged through his junk drawer, found an almost used up roll of duct tape and fashioned a crude handle out of it. He attached it in the center and without much effort, it came right out.

Sitting in a very shallow cavity was a thin, handwritten diary whose leather cover had begun to crack and tear. When he saw the gold leaf initials, JF, it caused him to audibly gasp. He stared at it at length, holding it with both hands. This was his father's diary, written in his own hand. This was big. He set it down, almost afraid to open it. Beneath the book was a small 8mm metal film canister. He took it out and placed it on the table and then gently pried the lid open. It seemed to be in remarkable shape. A touch brittle perhaps, but all things considered it looked rather good.

He turned back to the book. With one last pull on his beer, he hunched over it and carefully opened to page one. Except page one was not page one. The first few pages had been torn out- how long ago and what they contained was anyone's guess, but John began to read it out loud. It was his way to somehow bring it more to life- he wanted to hear it as well as comprehend it.

"*There is a refusal on the part-*" John stopped and actually blurted out "This was...It's my dad!" still struggling with the magnitude of what he was doing. He took a breath and continued.

"*There is a refusal on the part of any bureaucrat to even consider anything other than hard, empirical data as the cause for this society's incredible abilities. And so that's what we have given them. We've filled our official reports with copious amounts of flora and fauna examinations, diet and nutritional habits and sleep patterns. All of which mean nothing. The concern is that they may tire of our inconclusive conclusions and replace the team before we've had a chance to master the fundamentals. The French have already sent in an observer and I suspect it is just a matter of time before the Americans do as well. It should be noted that we have made some progress, albeit small, in our own abilities. We have managed to grow an entire row of breadfruit without any water whatsoever. Not exactly the grand Koontal of the elders, but impressive nonetheless. I am optimistic*

that my ability to operate Koontal will begin to increase exponentially. It feels like a muscle that gets stronger with each day. I'm a scientist so all this goes against all that I am to reach the conclusions we've reached. It is its simplicity that is the most baffling and the reason it is so elusive. Believing is receiving. Nearly impossible for us to comprehend and execute because our knowledge promotes doubt- we trust in the five senses. Not these people. Their world is a world of magical simplicity. Life lived in the absence of doubt. And that is key. We westerners see this on rare occasions usually because of absolute dire circumstances that demand a supernatural answer. Somehow here that component is not a requirement and the impossible is done on a daily basis- I suspect simply because they don't know they can't."
It was signed John Ferrum Sr.

John went back and read the passage a second time. This time more slowly, like a well-crafted pour-over coffee, stopping every couple of sentences to give the words time to filter down and be fully absorbed. There was both comfort and a completion of sorts in the words. For the first time he felt a confirmation of his own outlook and began to sense that his lifelong curiosity, a curiosity that had gnawed at him for so long, was about to be satisfied. Someone else understood him. More importantly someone else shared his bizarre experience that till now, was so difficult to even put into words. As much as he continued to deny the events that made him different as a kid, this somehow allowed him to finally accept and embrace his knowledge of his own unique abilities. Just the admission in using those words to describe himself- *"unique abilities"* was groundbreaking. The simple act of reading something written decades ago, by someone he hardly knew- for John, the discovery was nothing short of exhilarating.

He laid the book back down, much the way one would pause during an incredible meal to savor the moment. He picked up the film canister again and gently unrolled a short length of film. He held it up to the kitchen light but the tiny frames of the 8mm film revealed little. He was going to need a projector and he just so happened to know who had one.

He left his apartment and walked down the hall. He stopped briefly as he neared the last door on the left. The muffled sounds of explosions, gunfire and screeching tires told him that Max was home. John knocked on the door. A Latino voice yelled out, "Whatchu wan wit me!"

"Yeah, hey is Max there?" John yelled back. " I just want to-"

"He gonna beat yo ass, floor it!" another voice shot back. More gunfire.

"Ohhh..." he laughed, "GTA."

John let himself in. There was Max, headphones on, sitting on his avocado green Goodwill couch, Grand Theft Auto on the flat screen, completely oblivious to John's presence behind him.

"Hey Max- Just gonna borrow that old projector... and this box of doughnut holes......and... your wallet. By the way, your couch is on fire. Later dude!"

He grabbed the projector, stuffed a doughnut hole in his mouth and let himself out. Back in his apartment he placed the projector on a box and plugged it in. Because of John's penchant for 'minimalist' design, it wasn't hard to find a blank wall to use as a screen. After carefully threading the old film through the sprockets, he doused the light and sat down in his ratty plaid recliner with Max's box of half-eaten, leftover donut holes. He paused briefly, nodded to himself in preparation and flipped the projector on.

It sprang to life with a bit of a clatter but there on the wall before him was the moving picture version of the photo he had discovered first in Miss Edna's cockpit and now in Professor Wharton's crate. Everyone and everything awash in that amber light that was common to 30-year-old, 8mm home movies. Everyone was happy and clowning as they gathered for what would become a popular group photo. As the camera panned about, John recognized some of the terrain as well as a much shinier, newer Miss Edna in the background perched on the dirt airstrip alongside its bamboo cousin, the villagers' replica P-38.

There were random shots of researchers, foliage, closeups of monkeys gnawing at stolen food- all unedited and without any coherence or chronology. Suddenly Sam's face filled the screen. He looked exactly the same.

"Was he ever young?" John jokingly asked himself.

Sam was being prepared for an interview. John recognized the backdrop used in the 1976 National Geographic documentary that Professor Wharton had shown the class as part of its discussion on the Cargo Cult. The much younger, then Chief Sam wore his trademark smile as the pompous, condescending correspondent asked the now memorable question, "Really chief, isn't it a bit foolish to continue waiting for your Messiah? After all, it's been over seventy years now." And without missing a beat he answered,

"No. No more foolish than you Christians who waiting for yours for *two thousand* years."

"Yes!!"

John loved that mic-drop moment from the first time he heard it but even more so now that he knew Sam and Sam's big heart. Sam described the simple life they had and how the early colonists nearly destroyed it. He went on to explain how the American GIs were different. They were kind and caring. Most importantly, the tribe saw that dark men, men who looked like them, were treated as equals, working, and living side by side with the white man. It was then they knew that their messiah would come from such a group of people. And of course, there were the wondrous toys they brought with them. But they suddenly vanished and the magical stuff they'd come to know and love went with them.

"This simple life, this utopian existence you speak of... do you have *any* problems? Surely you must have some..." the correspondent surmised.

"Yes," Sam said. "Ratumu drink much Kava and he forget to tie canoe and wave come and take canoe away."

"That's all, that's it?" he asked. He laughed. "That's your biggest problem?"

"Oh, no," Sam said. "Ghosts. Giants come. They take women away. That very sad."

The correspondent looked at his cameraman with a snarky smirk. With that, the footage of Sam's National Geographic interview abruptly stopped, and the screen was now filled with more close-up plant samples and random scenery. John's focus once again shifted back to the stacks of papers.

Sifting through the last stack of stuff he came across a tiny picture paper-clipped to an entrance application. It was for a prep school in Hawaii and was only partially filled out. The name on the report had been scrawled in as Emerald, but the space for a last name had been left blank. If John wasn't mistaken, this was the same little girl he first noticed in all the other group shots. Then it hit him. This was the 5-year-old version of the 'EM' Professor Wharton wanted him to meet with. Who was she? What "answers", as Professor Wharton put it, would she have? Answers about Nephilim? His past? His family? That's it! The comments, her placement in the photos- he was rapidly putting the pieces of the puzzle together and he was inevitably drawn to the only conclusion that made sense to him.

"Oh my God, a sister!" he said out loud. "*My* sister!? No doubt a brainiac. Ugh, great. This won't be *too* awkward."

He sat there pondering the idea of their upcoming meeting and whether *she* knew for that matter.

He was about to turn the projector off when another figure appeared on the screen. It was the face of a beautiful woman who, judging by the odd angle and poor lighting, had hastily placed the camera on the nearest flat surface and began filming herself. Her eyes were wild, her face wearing a plethora of emotions- she seemed distraught, panicked yet resigned and a tad crazed from the choice she was being forced to make. She paused, looking at the ceiling as if searching for the words, searching for divine guidance.

"I can't do this..." she said.

John's eyes grew wide in sudden realization. He knew this woman. This was the woman he saw in his recurring, never ending dream. This was the woman he ran back to in the face of all that peril. This was his mother.

"Your father has been gone in the interior for months. Men came and took him. To question him. Ghost giants raided the village twice taking three of the young women. Jesus, they shredded six goats for sport!"

Tears began rolling down her face. She quickly collected herself.

"Now we're going into hiding. It's so dangerous and getting worse. The watchers are stirring up the tribe, thanks to that fuck Howard." She gasped at her vulgar slip and covered her mouth.

"I don't know, I don't know what to do. Chances are, if you're viewing this, I wasn't able to achieve Koontal- at least not enough to get myself out of this," she said, shaking her head. Her eyes darted about the room. A touch more panic beginning to take hold. John could feel her panic as if it were his own.

"I just can't stop the fear! It's probably not good. We didn't abandon you, we had to send you away. Keep you safe. Because we love you. So much. So, so much.... I want to die. Dear God, first little Em and now you. I Promise, I promise I'll come for you! If the unthinkable were to happen, start with the three royal chieftains. We think they're buried in Ohio." She laughed but it was somewhat a crazed laugh "Jesus, Ohio!"

At this point it was as if she had forgotten the camera was recording and she was just talking to herself.

"Oh God, that's not gonna mean anything. You can't understand now but one day you will. One day you will stare down the impossible and it may seem overwhelming, but you will overcome the circumstances - never, ever doubt that. You will my sweet. I promise." She glanced away and smiled sweetly.

"Every day you would bring me a shell. It was such a sweet thing- I kept everyone, everyone as if it were treasure... because to me, it surely was. I kept them in this satchel. My precious boy. But now I have to go- I'll keep them with me always until I can put them back in your precious little hands when-"

The film boiled and broke.

Wiping away his tears, John frantically tried to feed the film back into the projector but to no avail. That was it. That's all there was. He froze momentarily, in a light bulb moment and then suddenly began rummaging through his backpack. Frantically pulling the contents out and finally just dumping everything out on the table. There it was. The very satchel that his mom was holding in the film, the very one that was slung around his neck as he came out of the interior, filled with miniature nautilus shells. Holding it in his hand again triggered a sudden flood of memories. Memories of his time spent in the interior and the very circumstances surrounding his mom giving the satchel to him.

Bam! Bam! Bam! Bam! The pounding on the door startled him, interrupting his recollections.

"Ferrum!" a voice bellowed from the other side of the door. It was Max. John gathered himself and prepared to open the door.

"Ferrum!!" This time even more adamantly. "I want my doughnuts, Ferrum! Do not deny it, I know you were there. I could smell your..." Max was trying to find the right word. John opened the door. "... cleanliness!" Max said.

"I don't know what you're talking about." John said, blocking the door. Max tried to look past John and into his apartment to catch him in his lie, but John mirrored his every movement, blocking his view of the now empty doughnut box.

"When ya' get back?" Max asked. "I heard you didn't get the message until you were already gone so how'd it go? Did you hook up with any of the island chicas, did you have fun, did you? Did you see any chicks that I mighta hooked up with? Glad you're back! Bring it in, bro!" Max enveloped John in a bear hug raising him up leaving John's feet dangling above the floor. He turned him in the doorway enough to see the empty box on the table.

"Oh man! Did you finish all the holes? All of them? That was dinner! How do you steal a man's dinner and still live with yourself? And is that my projector? What are you, some thug who steals from his friends to support his drug habit?" John was now laughing.

"Well, you won't get much for it- bought it on Craigslist two years ago and it's never worked. Ever! Lost a ten spot on that deal. Why don't cha give me ten bucks for it, and I won't press charges on the doughnuts. Hey! Where ya goin'? It is a Dunkin' run!"

"Lock up will ya'?" John shouted back at Max as he headed down the hall.

"Where ya' goin'?" Max asked again.

John paused as he put his hand on the door.

"I'm goin' to get my mom."

The door swung open, and John stepped into the cool night.

CHAPTER 12

ROAD TRIP TO THE THREE CHIEFTAINS

E than had just gotten off his shift at the University's sleep center. His new job involved spending four hours watching other classmates sleep and record brainwave activity as they dreamt. It was a requirement for his post grad degree but the real reason, truth be known, was Emily Stroud. Watching Emily Stroud sleep on an antiquated black and white monitor was about as good as it got for Ethan. It was also about as close as he would ever get to spending any time in the sheets with her.

Ethan's hand was on the door of his new Nissan Cube when John's 16-year-old Volvo 850R rattled and groaned to a stop in the space next to him.

"Yo! Brotha', wazzup?!" Ethan said as he leaned back on his Cube.

"Ya' know," John said, pointing at him, "It's gettin' better. Gettin' better. That sounded authentically black."

Ethan scowled and slowly raised his hoodie up. With a deadpan look and in his best gangsta voice he threatened John.

"I will cut chu." Completely unfazed John moved the convo along. "How's Emily?"

"Oh dude, I think I'm really starting to communicate with her- telepathically of course."

"Of course." John replied.

"I mean about 20 minutes into her REM cycle I started putting out my vibe, ya' know, and she honest to God started thrashing. Proof positive, my friend. She wants me. She wants me bad. I mean it was- You don't care, do you?"

"Ehh, not so much." They both laughed.

"So, when did you get my text that the trip was delayed?" asked Ethan.

"Right when I got back...to civilization...and Wi-Fi," laughed John.

"Oh man, I am sooo sorry. Jay said it's supposed to happen late next week. It's messed up... a whole forty-foot container's worth of baby formula just sittin' on that runway in that hot sun. What a waste... you still in?"

"Oh, yeah. Hey, what do you know about Nephilim?" John asked.

"Wait, what? What went on over there? I haven't seen you since-"

"It's a long story- an extremely long, weird.... loooong story that I promise I will tell you- but first, what do you know about Nephilim?"

"Nephilim?" Ethan replied. "Oooo spooky time. Yeah. Giants...... giants from Biblical times. Why?"

"I might've just seen one."

Ethan looked away, then looked side to side the same way someone does when they're about to make a politically incorrect comment, assuring no one else was close enough to hear.

"Oh! yeah, ugh.... hmmmm. Ya' might just want to keep that to yourself. You're not still on that night at the Witch, are ya'?"

"No. Yeah, no, not really. What, what exactly are they?"

"Besides real scary?" Ethan answered. "Descendants of Satan dude. Fallen angels. Deep stuff here."

"Yeah?" John looked at him, waiting for him to continue.

"See, when Satan branched out on his own with his little... corporate takeover, thinking he could do a better job of creation than God? About a third of the angels went with 'em. It didn't take 'em long to discover what we all know- earth chicks are hot. And what girl can resist a bad boy angel, eh John?"

John smirked and rolled his eyes.

"Before long everybody's knockin' boots doin' the monkey dance and, voile'... the spawning of Nephilim. Big dudes, big, big, very powerful- not too bright but crazy strong. Remember David and Goliath? Well, there 'ya go. Nephilim. Really mean Nephilim too. Before long you've got the buggers all over the place... all according to plan."

"According to plan. Whose plan is that?" John asked.

"Da' debil missa John!" Ethan said in his ever-convincing Flip Wilson voice. "Satan's no dummy. He knew that the Messiah- the one who was gonna ultimately kick his evil ass all the way back to the gates of hell- had to come from the human bloodline. Well, if he could muddy the gene pool enough- Boom...problem solved! That's why God sent the great flood- you know Russell Crowe- built that big-ass ark and all the animals came?"

John looked confused.

"Noah?"

"Oh! Yeah, got it." John affirmed.

"Do you ever wonder why a loving God would instruct his people to go into a city and kill all the people? I mean all the people. Women, children- everybody? On the surface it doesn't make sense at all," Ethan said.

"Right."

"Makes God out to be an incredible dick, don't ya' think?

"Right."

"It's because they weren't human!" Ethan continued. "They looked human but were actually messed up half humans with polluted DNA. Hybrids. Whole different ball game once 'ya know that."

By this point John's mouth hung open in sheer amazement.

"How do you know all this stuff?" John asked.

"Sunday school. My dad made me go. Hated it."

"Well, wanna go see one?"

"One what?"

"Nephilim." John said matter of factly.

"Living or dead?"

"Dead."

"Yeah!" John opened the passenger door to his car.

"Get in."

Sixteen years ago, Volvo's weren't quite the luxury autos they are today. Spartan and utilitarian, like the Swedes who designed them, made them sturdy but not necessarily comfy. But sturdy was good, especially considering the roads leading to the dig site were a bit of 'Over the river and through the woods to Grandmother's house we go.' The Indian burial mounds were one of many sites, but this particular site was located along the Hockings River in Athens County, Ohio. They pulled up, the trail of dust finally catching up to them, engulfing the car in a heated, billowy brown cloud, John and Ethan made their way towards the largest of the three tents whose entrance was partially blocked by numerous large, wooden crates draped in faded, green canvas.

"Excuse me, can I help you guys?" inquired a heavy-set woman carrying a sifter full of small bone specimens.

"Yeah, we're here to see Em? I was told that-" The woman wasted no time in motioning with her head to the inside of the smaller tent and disappeared into the gigantic one. Ethan and John walked over, lifted the tan flap of the tent, and stood just inside the entrance giving their eyes a moment to adjust to the subdued lighting. It was only marginally cooler than the outside and air had that slightly stale, musty smell to it. Inside were two folding tables littered with hundreds of pottery shards, small bones and other oddities being readied for photographing. In the back corner was a young woman, working intently, busily examining a small artifact through a microscope.

"Dude! She's smokin' hot! Seriously!" Ethan whispered "Seriously shut up. Go look around- but don't touch anything!" John whisper-yelled, waving Ethan away. Ethan shot John an overly exaggerated indignant look and began to quietly sing the lyrics from *West Side Story's 'A Boy Like That'*.

"one of your own kind, stick to your own kind..." John shook his head, laughed, and motioned for him to shut up.

John walked over and pulled up a stool beside her. She didn't even glance at him.

"So, where's home for you?" John asked.

"Right now, it's in a Samsonite roll-away at the Efficiency Inn about 4 miles from here." she said without taking her eyes from the two lenses. "And you are?"

"John...Professor Wharton?... said we should meet? and there was something or some information you might be able to help me with?.... No, I mean where are you from?"

Her body slumped ever so slightly, her head cocked to one side in resignation as she looked up to see who this person was that had wandered in with the specific intent of interrupting her work. But that look quickly softened when she caught sight of him. She had been caught off guard, not expecting someone quite this handsome to suddenly appear next to her in her dusty tent. She was suddenly painfully aware that she had rushed out the door that morning without a stitch of makeup. Of all the mornings to forego just even a little eyeliner for heaven's sake... She immediately went into recovery mode, extending her hand.

I'm Em." she said as she pulled her long, black hair back. John smiled.

"John."

"I was raised in the South Pacific- a small island called Tanna in Vanuatu. What about you?"

"Well, I was raised by my Uncle in-"

"Oh my gosh! Really? Seriously? Em gushed. "So was I!"

John had to remind himself to go easy in his questioning. He wasn't sure how much of their common history she knew but it would be far more productive, and she would be far more forthcoming if it was all set in the context of just casual conversation between two new acquaintances.

"So, your parents were...?"

"My parents were part of a research team stationed on the island and well..." Em's voice trailed off and her expression quickly changed. She was suddenly serious and sad.

"They were taken," she said. Her eyes broke away from John's and were fixed on three large coffin-like crates at the far end of the tent. "They were taken away by.... them." motioning towards the crates. "Nephs. Not even sure why."

She turned back to the microscope. The bubbly schoolgirl was gone, and the serious archeologists had returned.

"Good going Ace," John thought. "Led her smack dab into a bad memory."

"That's why these guys are so important to me" she said while peering into the microscope.

"No one believed me as a child and... now we've got proof- sort of. It's a start anyway."

She looked back up and smiled mischievously. "Ever seen one before?"

"Maybe," John said. Em was surprised by his answer. "Not really sure but..."

"Well, did he have this?" Em pulled back the sheet covering his hand revealing six fingers.

"Whoa!" Ethan exclaimed from behind them. They both turned.

"Oh, Em, meet Ethan."

"Hey." Em continued, "That's how you can tell. I mean, there's a lot of big people in the world- not everyone's a Neph- but if they've got this?"

"How tall was this guy?" asked John.

"Guys." Em replied. "There's three of them and none of them are under 12 feet. 12 feet!"

"You think these guys are the three Royal Chieftains?"

Wow! I'm impressed. Yes, as a matter of fact I do," she said. "I'm in the minority on this but I think the Native Americans were trying to hide these guys, not exalt them. Ya' know how many identical mounds are out there? Remember in the old Westerns the Indians would always put up one hand," she put up a hand to demonstrate, "and say 'How!? Well, that wasn't some Hollywood invention. They were counting fingers- and showing five fingers back so that everybody knew what they were dealing with- good or evil. And from the way we found these guys? They definitely thought they were evil." One of the workers stuck his head in the tent.

"Hey Em! The guys from the Smithsonian are here."

"They're way too early!" she shot back. "I'm not done cataloging... they're not supposed to be here until late tomorrow!"

The worker shrugged and Em blew right by John and Ethan on her way to confront the driver. John and Ethan quickly followed behind her.

"Hey! Hey!" Em yelled trying to get the attention of the driver.

"Isn't she great? - she's awesome!" a mesmerized Ethan declared.

"Never. Mind!" Reel it in there, Kemosabe......but yeah," John smiled, "she is."

"Hey! You're way too early. I haven't even catalogued - I'm supposed to accompany them, I don't have any of my stuff..." Em was interrupted by the truck driver.

"Sweetheart, I got my paperwork. I have a boss; you have a boss- just doing what I'm told, and I was told to load these three big crates pronto. Sign here," he said, handing her a pen. Em ignored the pen and paperwork while the driver headed back towards the truck.

"Let me at least check the packing." As she struggled trying to lift the heavy lid, John and Ethan stepped forward to lend a hand. "There's something wrong here," Em said quietly as she poked and prodded at the crate's contents. John agreed.

"I'll say. Did you happen to notice his shoes?" "Not to mention how many delivery drivers do you know that wear a Patek Phillipe watch?" Ethan noted. Em was doing her best not to panic.

"I can pretty much guarantee that whatever the professor wanted you to, see?... is in that crate! What do we do?"

"We track 'em, that's what we do." John stated.

"Just how do we do that?"

"Ethan's gonna drop his burner flip-phone in the box and then do his super sleuth thing."

"I am?" a surprised Ethan said. John shook his head and whispered in Em's ear.

"Drug dealers pffft. Have to admit- he fits the profile." He winked and turned back to Ethan. "You've got your app runnin' right?"

Yeah."

"Make sure you turn the ringer off. You know, in case ET here decides to phone home..."

Ethan hesitated and was not happy. At all.

"Dude," Ethan said through his teeth, "you know this isn't any old flip phone, it's-"

"Come on! We'll get your transponder back there Scotty as soon as we get out of here." John turned

away from Em and shot a look towards Ethan and whispered "Look, your gonna have to field test your app at some point... might as well be today, right?" Ethan reluctantly silenced the phone and handed it to John. John in turn slipped it deep into the folds of the crate's packing materials. John turned to Ethan and said, "Here are my keys. Gas up the car and I'll go with Em to get her stuff. Meet back here in forty-five. They're probably not gonna need more than an hour or so to finish crating these bad boys up.

Em threw her backpack towards the spot where a back seat should have been of her open-air Jeep and banged through the gears like an Indy pro. As she needled her way through the dusty two-lane road, she continued shaking her head. John, smart enough to remain silent, shot glances her way, watching her work through her frustration at a hair raising 65 MPH. Looking straight ahead she said to herself, "Breathe. It'll work out, it'll work out." With that she turned to John and half smiled as the wind sufficiently buffeted them.

"So... raised by your uncle too huh? Your parents- they still around? I mean- what's the story?"

"Eh... a bit like yours, I guess. Foggy details, bits and pieces but I've got to admit I spend a lot more time than I should lately trying to figure it all out." John confessed.

"Ah - preachin' to the choir on that one. I've made a career out of trying to figure it all out."

"For what it's worth, I'd like to help," John said. Em smiled.

"At least you knew who your parents were - are," John said. "For me it's just bits and pieces that I've been able to pry out of people. After all these years you'd think... I dunno. Why all the mystery, ya' know?"

"No one will ever understand why we need answers," Em said. "I guess it's a bit like riding Harley's. Ya' know if you have to ask you wouldn't understand?"

"Yeah, I'm not even sure why it's so important at this point. Probably should just get on with it but I just recently came across- Whoa!" A startled John quickly reached up and grabbed the padded roll bar.

Em swung into the parking lot almost on two wheels, Tokyo drifting into a just barely adequate parallel parking spot. Mere inches from the curb, Em looked around checking.

"Am I...?"

"Oh Yeah, yeah! Were-We're good!" a wide-eyed John replied looking down on the less than 2-inch gap between the tire and the curb.

Em inserted the key and the orange door swung open. She quickly turned the window AC on as the motel room air was stale and plopped her keys on the generic, Formica dresser. There were stacks of paperwork and books on the nightstand next to the bed, a small bag of picks and hammers- all the stuff you would imagine a workaholic archeologist would have strewn about. It was not the tidiest of places and it seemed to cause Em a bit of embarrassment.

"Oh, yeah, mmm. Oops," Em said as she began picking up stray clothes.

"Here, let me give you a hand," John said as he began to pitch in.

"Sorry, wasn't exactly expecting guests."

John glanced around and charitably offered, "I was thinking it kinda feels like home."

Em looked over at him. Her gaze immediately lowered to his hands. He in turn looked down as well. Wasn't this awkward. Without realizing it, helpful John had picked up and was holding a very sexy, bright blue bra.

"Feels like home?" she repeated. A flustered John sheepishly handed it back to her.

"Think I'll just... use your, um, restroom if that's OK."

"Sure. You're gonna feel like you've gone home for the holidays in there," she said with a wry smile. "Hang on, just let me..." The bathroom, looking like a Victoria Secret storeroom, was filled with brightly colored, very sexy underwear hanging from every surface.

"Oh," John managed to mutter.

"Make some room for you..." Em finished her thought.

John shut the door and stared at himself in the mirror. Standing there in silence he shut his eyes, held his head, and silently screamed, "*Fuuuuuuuuuuuuuuuk*!!!" He opened his eyes and lectured himself, "Remember!! Sister! Sister!!'" He quickly regained his composure and came back out just in time to see Em putting a feathery, white costume into a garment bag. The same feathery costume that he had seen his dream caretaker seductively dancing in during the Kava ceremony back on the island. He immediately whipped around and went back into the bathroom and shut the door. "This just keeps getting weirder and weirder," he thought. He looked heavenward and then immediately came back out again. Em looked at him with a half-smile, waiting for an explanation for that move.

"Forgot to put the seat down," John said nervously. "Bringing your pet rooster?"

"This? Oh, it's a ceremonial costume my grandmother made. It's supposed to be used only in marriage because the dance is a little...I suppose...provocative. It's silly really."

"Oh no it's not! I, I mean you're...I, I'm sure you're a wonderful dancer. You're not married right?"

"No. You?"

"Oh no."

"Girlfriend? Boyfriend?" Em asked.

John laughed. "Nope... to all the aforementioned. I'm actually a lesbian trapped in a man's body."

"Perfect. I'm a gay man trapped in a woman's body. See? We have so much in common already," Em laughed.

"I'll say," added John. "And you have no idea just how much," he thought.

Long car rides can make fast friends or lifelong enemies. The conversations that ensue to pass the time are often stories of one's past and this was no exception. Ethan spent a great deal of time talking about his childhood, growing up black and affluent and the guilt that came with that. His father was a patent attorney, his mother a neonatal neurologist, which meant money was never a problem, but it also meant they were rarely home, leaving Ethan to figure out just where he fit in in an all-white, upper crust neighborhood. John had a natural affinity for him since the day they met. Probably because like him, his childhood was uniquely challenging and different and rather than allowing it to become a deficit causing him to wallow in victimhood, it became the very thing that propelled him forward, molding him into the extraordinary guy he was. Whatever struggle Ethan was going through, whatever insecurities he had failed to purge in his youth, John made sure to make fun of it, never allowing him the luxury of leaning on it as any kind of an excuse.

John, however, was guarded in his answers and storytelling. He had adopted a healthy skepticism towards everyone and everything ever since that freakish night. He was unsure of Em's awareness to the possible family connection and didn't want to tip his hand quite yet. There was also the matter of her involvement in the village. It was clear there were two factions within the community- the happy go lucky ones and the somewhat creepy, sinister ones. Until he was sure, really sure which group she fit in with, he needed to determine whether she was trustworthy or not- no matter how hot she was. And there was the whole sister thing. It was turning out to be quite a confusing kettle of fish. He was especially careful not to mention that he and Em had in fact, actually met before and just how recent that meeting was. He hadn't been on his best behavior while in Tanna. As a matter of fact, he had been mostly either comatose or a drunken idiot whenever she was present, and he wasn't keen on reminding her of that guy. At least not until he had a chance to show her his better side. He prayed the white ash paint job he wore on the island had preserved his anonymity. He owed her an immense debt of gratitude and was looking forward to the day he could thank her properly, but today was not that day.

They arrived in DC just in time to join the lunch time crush clogging the sidewalks. It was noisy, filled with the sound of cars, conversations, accelerating buses and distant horns. It was the welcome sound of life being lived. It was a beautiful, sunny day and like most public spaces, there was no shortage of tourists and street entertainers and vendors scattered about. As the trio made their way up the steps of the Smithsonian, Em veered off, her attention drawn to one odd character in particular. Ethan and John stopped and watched from behind. As best they could tell, this street urchin had combined three popular panhandling themes. An end-of-the-world preacher, a guitar-playing Elvis impersonator and a three card Monty magician. From the looks of things, his sad, ill-fitting costume had probably lived its long life having never seen the inside of a dry cleaners.

"Best keep our distance. Not sure he's had all his shots," John joked.

"That's what I like about you John. Your infinite well of compassion," Ethan chided him, shaking his head.

"And upon his return he will find a greaaaat evil," he proclaimed loudly. "He will need to put on the whole armor of the Almighty. But especially the shield of faith. It is through that great faith that he shall close the door on evil incarnate!!" He proceeded to strike an iconic Elvis pose and held it. He turned, looked directly at Em and sneered asking, "Card trick? You there, pretty lady! Come forward." As Em made her way forward through the modest crowd, he played walking music on his beat up Silvertone guitar.

"Pick a card! But first," he showed the deck to his audience, "someone examine the deck- you!" He handed the deck to a sweaty tourist who was in a race with his melting ice cream cone. He nodded, confirming the deck was legit. "Alright then, go ahead, pick a card- don't show me! Show everybody else."

Em picked a card, showed it to the crowd and held it against her chest. It was the ten of hearts. Elvis then held the deck to his forehead and began to make proclamations.

"You seek answers, yes?" he asked.

"Don't we all?" Em responded with a smile. John and Ethan made their way forward to collect Em.

"You seek someone of great stature." Elvis still had the deck pressed against his forehead.

"Well, it's not this guy," said Ethan pointing at John.

"He holds a great secret, yes?" Em continued to nod at Elvis's comments but there was a hint of suspicion beginning to form in her eyes. Elvis continued, "Hidden for a long time this.... article you seek?"

Ethan leaned over and quietly said to John, "Am I the only one that just got a whiff of Yoda there?"

"And yet it has been in plain sight. Maybe the answer lies in these cards," he said as he lowered the deck from his forehead. Elvis then had someone from the crowd shuffle his deck and then asked another person to draw a card and show it to the onlookers. It was the ten of hearts. He then asked Em to show her card to the crowd. It was no longer the ten of hearts but rather the card simply read, Luke 6:45. The crowd reacted with both amazement and confusion.

"Well, that's not right," said Elvis. He took his well-worn bible, quickly turned to the passage, and began reading out loud in his better than average Elvis voice.

"A good man out of the good treasure of his heart brings forth good; and an evil man out of the evil treasure of his heart brings forth evil. For out of the abundance of the heart his mouth speaks..."

He then asked the man in the crowd to fan the cards out and show the crowd. The entire deck was now the ten of hearts.

"An abundance of hearts, get it?" he said while displaying his Elvis curled lip smile. "Show 'em your card again lil' darlin.'"

Em slowly revealed her card and her mouth dropped open. She turned it around and showed the crowd the ten of hearts. "Elvis has left the building!" He announced and he vanished in a giant puff of white smoke. The crowd's reaction was what one would expect- total shock and amazement. Everyone broke into applause. John and Em however exchanged a knowing look. This was no ordinary street entertainer who 'happened' to be there. For that matter, this was no ordinary magic either.

"There's a note," Em said as she stepped forward to the spot where Elvis had vanished.

"What's it say," asked John.

"*They will reveal the timetable by speaking to you from beyond the grave. For I have etched it upon his heart.*" Lastly a series of numbers was written- "*15230.*"

"You don't think he means.... literally, do you?" John queried.

"Manuscripts," Em stated. "Oftentimes notes to loved ones, property lists, and such would be placed in the most sacred of places of the dead. The heart. I never got the chance to examine his heart because-"

"Dapper Dan with the delivery van showed up early," Ethen interjected.

"Yes!!" Em exclaimed.

"So, what we're looking for is in..."John hesitated.

"The big dude's heart!" Ethan said.

"Ughh! how are we gonna get that?" John grimaced.

"Leave that to me," Em said. "I'm the girl with skills and a bag full of tools," she shook her backpack. It sounded like someone had stolen all the silverware from dinner. "You guys just have to get me in there."

They decided the best course of action was to go inside the main lobby and Ethan would check the coordinates that his flip phone had been pumping out ever since it had been placed inside the crate. It was programmed to send coordinates every 3 minutes only when it was on the move and to conserve power, cease sending if it remained in the same position for more than 30 minutes. The last send was over an hour and 40 minutes ago which meant, more than likely it had reached its final destination.

Inside, the three did their best to blend in with the tourists and day visitors. It was a cavernous, marble lined interior, three stories high with soaring arched windows at the very top. The lobby was nearly empty of exhibits except for an enormous elephant mounted on a pedestal made to look like something right out of his natural habitat in the center in the room.

"Well?" John asked with his eyes. Ethan held up a finger as he squinted in concentration, studying his phone's screen. He looked up and then around with a puzzled look on his face.

"That's odd…" he said.

"What's odd? John asked.

"Well, according to this… it should be…" Ethan looked around and behind him, "right here," he said pointing towards the massive elephant.

"Well look who it is," Em said. "I knew it!" The delivery driver who insisted on taking the crates early was walking towards the center of the room but now dressed very differently. He was in an expensive suit, carrying a leather valise and was directing some of the museum staff. Em started towards him intent on confronting him only to have John grab her arm and reign her in.

"Whoa! Easy killer. No need to tip our hand just yet."

"That briefcase," Ethan said, "My dad had the very same one. Stupid expensive. Guarantee, that's one of the guys we saw in the alley outside of the Witch!"

John stared at the floor trying to make sense of it. Way too many coincidences to be coincidences. There were connections everywhere and he had somehow fallen into each and every one of them. Where was it all leading? Wouldn't it be a lot easier just to forget everything and go back to being regular, student guy John? But in his heart of hearts, he knew that was no longer an option.

"The absence of alternatives clears the mind marvelously," John said to no one in particular.

Em was puzzled. "What?"

"Henry Kissinger," John said, nodding. "Henry Kissinger said that. Whenever I realize I'm agonizing over a decision that in fact I have no choice? I say that to myself." He smiled at her, "Stop eavesdropping!"

"He's coming this way!" Ethan quickly bent down, pretending to tie his shoe.

"Dude, you're wearing loafers." John said quietly. Ethan's head didn't move.

The fashionable delivery driver continued walking directly towards them, but the humongous elephant exhibit was between them and blocked their view of his approach. He never reappeared prompting the trio to walk to the other side of the mastodon. Sure enough, disguised as a large rock there was a doorway which led to a downward spiral staircase.

"Down! That's it! They're here, right here, but they're down, they're down below us." Ethan realized.

"Shall we?" asked Em. John and Ethan looked around nonchalantly and followed her down the staircase. It led to a small, nondescript room, a series of hooks holding smocks and lab coats, the only decoration next to a solitary door. They pulled on the handle, but it was locked by a security keypad.

"Well, anybody bring their lock pick set?" asked John.

"That's the one thing I don't have but..." Em dug in her bag. "Ya' know, it's a long shot but..." She pulled out the paper from the street magician and punched in *1 5 2 3 0*. She grasped the handle, her eyes grew wide, she smiled. "We're in!"

That single, nondescript door however led to a massive warehouse filled to the ceiling with crates, sculpture, paintings- all in various stages of restoration and repair. This was obviously a work area normally filled with specialists and restoration artists, but it was lunch hour, and most were away from their workspaces.

"Look at all this! This is honestly the biggest warehouse I've ever been in. What now?" Em said softly.

"First we put these on." John handed each of them a grey lab coat. "Then we locate Ethan's phone. Activate your LuvBug thing."

"What luvbug thing?" Em asked.

"It's an app I developed," Ethan explained. "You enter a description of yourself, a description of your dream date and if the two of you happen to be within range....it lets you know that it's a match and the two of you are in the same area, even the same room. It works by using a combination of NFR and next-gen Bluetooth type thing. Pretty cool."

"Great. Booty call tools- just what we need," Em concluded, her eyes continuing to scan for the crates.

"Yeah, but this booty call is for some serious Nephilim love," defended Ethan with a smile.

"So, Ethan, me and my phone are just dreaming about a guy like you. What do I enter to describe you?" John asked him. "Give it to me exactly the way you entered it so that we're sure to get a match." Ethan was silent and suddenly had a deer-in-the-headlights look. "Hey, c'mon. How did you describe yourself? So, I can pinpoint your phone?"

"Ughh, alright..." Ethan let out a big sigh and with great reluctance began to recite the description he had entered for himself. "Tall, dark, athletic build with deep-set, bedroom eyes. Witty, humorous.... financially set Calvin Klein jeans model."

"Is that it? Sure, you didn't... cure any diseases or anything?" John said, shooting a look towards Em while holding back his laughter. John entered the info and activated the app.

"So, what now?" Em asked John.

"We scour the place and hope that Ethan's phone had a full charge. And the app actually works." They began going down each aisleway as quickly as possible, a difficult thing for Em to do as there were so many distractions.

"Oh! this is amazing! It's from the Paleozoic era!" Em gushed as she gingerly picked up a stone carving from the shelf. Ethan and John looked at each other nodding in complete agreement while completely clueless as to what in the world Em was talking about.

John couldn't resist. "Are you sure?"

"Yes, I'm sure! It's certainly not the Cenozoic. The Cenozoic spans only about 65 million years, from the end of the Cretaceous Period and the extinction of non-avian dinosaurs to the present."

"Certainly." Ethan's facetious deadpan expression caused John to bite his lip.

"Just so you know, you two are.... stupid. Stupid one and stupid two," she said, pointing at each of them. With that she turned on her heels, threw her head back and headed towards the back of the warehouse. Suddenly a door opened, and a worker wheeled a cart towards them. They quickly scrambled into the first available door and hid behind a line of file cabinets. The worker was collecting a few samples and stopped to look at his phone. John peered out the lone window in the door watching and waiting for him to move on.

"Geez," whispered Ethan. "Crop circles, the Bermuda Triangle, the lost Pyramids... is there any weirdness these guys weren't involved in?" He and Em were already passing the time by going through some of the file cabinets.

"When you understand just how strong these guys were? Building things like Stonehenge, the pyramids aren't so mysterious," Em whispered. "Just think what a bunch of them could do!"

"Amazing." Ethan said.

"Yeah. Amazingly scary. You'll never learn about their involvement in all sorts of unexplained things from any history books," Em added. John held a finger up to his lips. The worker had finally left but there was some activity in the adjacent room. He pointed towards the door. There was light coming from underneath it and shadows indicated someone was walking on the other side of it. The door swung open, and the trio got their first glimpse of one of the crates. Two men were prying open the lid with a crowbar. Once the lid was removed, another man approached and peered inside.

"Remember the alleyway? That's the same ugly giant- the one who disappeared!" John whispered. "And the same one at the airstrip. How can he get around so far so quick!? That's just impossible!"

"And the guy with the buzz?" Ethan noted, "Wait till he turns around- one hundred percent positive that's our delivery driver. I just remembered. He's the guy we saw the next day at-"

"The Red Witch, yes!" John finished his sentence.

The men began picking through the skeletal remains. The huge guy pulled out a small animal hide purse from its chest area where the heart had been and carefully opened it. There was a manuscript rolled up inside it.

"Out of the abundance of the heart..." Em mumbled.

"The mouth speaks," John answered her. "That's what we've been looking for. We've got to get that scroll."

"Mr. Howard?" a voice rang out from down the hall. "Call for you...in your office."

"*Fletcher* Howard!?" John quietly exclaimed. "Wharton warned me about this guy!"

The tall buzz cut Mr. Howard stuck his head out the door and yelled back, "Well, who is it?"

The hallway echoed with the clicking of heels as the chubby office assistant sauntered down the hall. Her hair was blonde, most of it anyway, with streaks of red matching her much too short polyester pencil skirt. Mr. Howard quickly stepped into the hallway shutting the door behind him and openly eyeballed her.

"What's in there that you don't want me to see?" she asked coyly, "Are you two-timing me?"

"And why would I do that?" he asked while looking to see if anyone was around. Satisfied, he reached out and grabbed a handful of her ample buttocks.

"Fletcher!" she feigned indignation. She slapped his hand, giggled, and began to walk away.

"You have a call?" she reminded him.

"Who is it?"

"Gerard Allen."

"That's Colonel Gerard Allen to you. He *so* likes the title," he added sarcastically. He followed the office tart down the long hallway to his office and shut the door. This was a two fisted, double uppercut to the jaw for John. Fletcher Howard, *the* Fletcher Howard taking a phone call from his uncle. What the hell!? What possible explanation could there be for that?

Fletcher Howard's windowless office sat at the far end of the warehouse, close to the loading dock and clearly did not match the upscale wardrobe he seemed to sport daily. It was tastefully decorated in all things beige, the only punch of color being a dusty gold and red 'Commendable Service' plaque hanging on the blank wall. He looked at the phone on his desk, pausing in a moment of reluctance before picking it up and punching the blinking hold button.

"Fletcher Howard!" he announced.

"Colonel Allen," barked the voice on the other end. It was indeed Gerard Allen; John's uncle and he was not happy. "What the hell took you so long? Look, we need to draw him in. The only way to do that is to bring his father out," he continued.

"We don't have his father, remember? We've got his mother, but they'd never let us take her out, even for this," a frustrated Fletcher shot back.

"Aren't you the guy who claims to have all this clout with those moron giants?" the colonel goaded him. "Anyway... We don't need them. He just has to think we've got him. You still have that crusty old pilot Aiden, don't you?"

"Yeah," Fletcher affirmed.

"Just dope him up and put the word out that John Ferrum is going on trial. That'll bring him in."

"Will do. Gerard? We just found it," Fletcher proudly announced.

"The Location? You've located the tupu horore?" the first sign of enthusiasm Gerard had shown for Fletcher's efforts.

"Well, not exactly but it won't be-"

CLICK.

"Long now." Fletcher slammed the phone. "You prick!" he muttered to himself.

Without warning, John's phone lit up and sounded the alarm. Ethan's LuvBug app had just found the perfect girl. He quickly stifled it. But was he quick enough? They all looked at each other in stunned silence trying to answer that question in each other's eyes.

Em peered back into the room where they were preparing to push the Nephilim remains into the furnace. The roar of the furnace as they opened the heavy, cast iron door seemed to have saved them. Ethan leaned against the wall breathing a sigh of relief- they had apparently gone unnoticed.

Suddenly the room exploded as a huge arm broke through the wallboard and wrapped itself around Ethan's neck. His horrified, wide eyed expression shocked Em and John into a momentary paralysis. In an instant, he was gone. It had pulled him back through the wall with such force that it created a hole larger than the actual doorway itself. Ethan's screams became muffled as the beast squeezed his neck with greater force. Em was first to jump through the hole, John following closely behind. She immediately launched into her college self-defense course yelling, "Eyes! Nose! Throat! Groin!" with each strike she made. It had no effect whatsoever on the giant and Ethan was beginning to turn red, gasping for air. John picked up a large wooden clamp from a nearby table and swung it onto the side of the beast's knee. It worked enough to drop the brute to one knee, but he still hadn't loosened his grip on Ethan's neck. With his other hand he grabbed a hold of John's collar and now both were in his clutches. Ethan clawed and bit with what little strength he had left and still he refused to let go. Em had run out of ideas and simply jumped on his back preparing to ride him like an agitated bull at the county fair rodeo. He struggled under the weight of three grown adults globbing themselves on to him but seemingly defying the laws of physics and all things normal, he was still able to stand. At the same time Em reached out and grabbed the closest thing available, a generous length of yellowed, gauzy fabric and wrapped it around his monstrous neck. For all she knew it could have been the Shroud of Turin but right then and right there it didn't matter a whit. She grabbed it, twisted it, wrapping it around her wrists and with all her might, reared back trying desperately to choke the very life out of him. She somehow managed to hoist herself up and wrap her legs around his neck, locking her ankles and was now dangling upside down on his enormous back. He began to spin attempting to throw them off. But not a normal turning- he was somehow able to spin himself beyond any earthly human capacity and the resulting centrifugal force quickly did its job. Ethan was the first to go. Em was next, flying off and across the floor and under a worktable .Her face contorted from the blow of hitting the wall. John was able to hang on a bit longer, but it certainly didn't help him any. He flew off even faster towards one of the shelving units holding several fifty-pound bags of plaster of Paris. He hit the front leg of the shelving unit with his shoulder hard enough that the leg snapped, causing the shelving unit to list to one side like a badly leaking ship and began dumping the heavy bags one by one directly onto John's head. John was now curled up on the floor, unconscious and covered in a mountain of white dust. Again.

The Neph, now free of his human baggage, stood staring at the white lump John had become and squinted while shaking his head, trying to clear his dizziness. For the first time he was vulnerable. Ethan and Em both knew it and without hesitation took a shot. Without so much as a word, Ethan looked at Em, looked at the huge furnace and in an instant shoved the gurney into the backs of his oversized legs. At the same time, Em leapt from her hiding spot and in midair, grabbed two handfuls of his thick, black hair slamming his head down onto the metal gurney. With one final push, Em lept from the gurney. The Neph still on his back, rolled into the fiery furnace and disappeared in the flames. The horrific sound of a large, screaming animal pierced the dusty air and went on for what seemed like an eternity. Em used a metal broom handle to close the red-hot door hoping to stifle the screams. Sparks and embers swirled as she managed to slam the door shut.

"What the...What was.... You said these guys were dead!!?

"Grab the valise! It's got the scroll in it," Em shouted at Ethan. She immediately went to John who had since come to and was holding his head, moaning.

"Floating access points. Certain times, certain locations," John muttered almost incoherently. "I remember."

Em knelt on the floor, staring in disbelief at the now white John. John met her gaze. "What?"

"Oh my God!" she said. She instinctively recoiled, dropping his head the few inches to the floor. "I remember too! You were there!" she said pointing at him, "You're... you're John Frum!"

"Geez, not you too!" said John in exasperation. But Em's expression was not one of admiration and awe so often displayed by the villagers of Tanna but one of downright disdain and betrayal.

Suddenly the fire suppression system came on soaking the trio.

"We've got to go!" Ethan yelled at the pair over the piercing alarm bells.

"Here's our chance," John told them. "Quick, Em, grab the valise. We can blend in with everyone else. They'll be looking for three. Ethan, you head out the loading dock. Keep your head down and make your way home. I'll call first chance we get. Em and I'll ditch the lab coats, head upstairs and head out with the rest of the tourists. Go!"

As John and Em emerged out into the cavernous lobby, the chaotic crowd surged towards the front doors. Two men stood head and shoulders above the crowd and were holding a photograph and frantically scanning the mass of people. They were looking for someone. In all likelihood, them. The indoor downpour worked in their favor however, turning everyone's hairdo into the same sloppy mess. The pair covered their faces and heads with their guide maps and scurried to the door, being sure to bunch up with a group of ninth graders on a field trip.

"Stay together everyone!" Em shouted, doing her best to sell their disguise. Soon they found daylight, heading down a block to snag a cab ahead of the soaking crowd.

CHAPTER 13

FUN WITH SOMEONE ELSE'S MONEY

Located deep within the Smithsonian's basement warehouse, a group of uniformed security guards scrambled to make sense of the alarm. They stood huddled around a tremendous bank of CCTV monitors when the door suddenly burst open. A frantic Fletcher Howard headed straight for them.

"Move!!" he yelled.

In his hand was a single, blurry photograph. It looked eerily similar to the famous striding BigFoot photo that had been proffered over the years as the irrefutable proof of its existence. Except this Big Foot was white and the size of a normal man. And happened to be John. The covered in white ash John. It had been hastily snapped in the jungles of Tanna during the Kava ceremony by some of Fletcher's henchmen, the same ones who followed Marco into the jungle and remained the only photo Fletcher had of him.

"I need to review the tapes," he snapped. "Take me back to just before the sprinklers went off. Wait! Stop! Ok, back it up- there!" The guard freeze-framed the image of John, Em and Ethan entering the warehouse hallway. John had struck the exact same pose.

"Zoom in." He held the photo next to the screen. "Well look who it is. The Messiah. Right here among us...and... with my valise." Fletcher opened his laptop and began scanning the screen.

"Where you goin' oh, chosen one?" he muttered to himself. "Don't you love technology? There! They're head west on Constitution."

By now, the street was clogged with people and the flashing lights of emergency vehicles of every description making it even more difficult for John to hail a cab. After an unsuccessful five minutes, Em had had enough, grabbed John's arm, pulled him away from the curb and backed him up against the building like an elementary school child being put in time-out.

"Stand here, outta sight." she said. She took off her soaked hoodie, wrapped it around her waist revealing an equally drenched white T-shirt. She inserted two fingers into her mouth and produced an ear shattering whistle. Two yellow cabs nearly collided clamoring to be the first to get over to the curb. Words were exchanged between the cabbies until one of them ended the conversation by raising the one finger salute and quickly speeding off.

"This is us," she said. Soaked, but a grateful Em climbed in clutching the valise while a somewhat dumbfounded John followed her into the back seat.

"The Westin-Georgetown," John told the driver. He turned to Em whose mood had taken a turn for the worse ever since her discovery of John's alter ego. She refused to even meet his glance, choosing instead to stare out the side window. He looked over at her and in hushed tones began to explain himself.

"Look, I umm...was going to say something...uh...when, when the time was right." Em was not having it and her expression was that of pure deadpan.

"*I* haven't even figured this all out yet myself. Everybody's convinced I'm something or someone I'm not. I've got a whole bunch of people who want me dead or worse and I haven't even been able to understand why- I haven't even told Ethan, uh...I got a little caught up in everything on the island, I really didn't mean to.... well...so... I'm sorry. I'm *really* sorry."

Em continued looking straight ahead, unfazed, and expressionless. They both sat, in awkward silence, looking straight ahead for what seemed like forever. John leaned in closely.

"You really are a good dancer though." he said quietly, an ear-to-ear grin slowly forming on his face. "I mean damn, girl! Day-uum!"

Em hauled off and punched him in the shoulder. She slowly looked over at him, her expression unchanged. She slowly turned away to look out her window. But in the faint reflection of the glass, John caught a glimpse of an ever so slight smile on her face. It was all the confirmation he needed that all was right again and like a big brother, put his finger in her ear. She jumped and giggled just as they pulled up in front of the hotel. Em quickly jumped out leaving John to pony up the cab fare. As John placed the bills in the cab driver's hand, he noticed something. Specifically, something peculiar about his hand.

Em was already halfway through the revolving doors and headed for the front desk. John caught up to her.

"Walk with me." he said, grabbing her under her arm and gently veering her towards the lobby's back entrance.

"Hey! where are you going?" she quietly protested. "They have cucumber water! Let's check in! Come on, it's on our new friend..." she began checking out the wallet in the valise, "uhh... Fletcher Howard- good 'ol Fletch! Geez! There's gotta be... at least a thousand bucks in here!" Pulling her aside, he plucked the wallet from her and studied the name.

"Notice anything suspicious about our cab driver? Anything?"

"Like what?" she asked.

"Well, I dunno, his size for one?"

"Yeah, he was big, but like I said, not every big guy is a Neph ya' know."

"Did you see his hands? Did you see the two scars on the sides?" John motioned to his own hands, "like something had been *removed*?"

Em gasped. "The sixth finger! Oh, my Go-"

"Yeah...HOW!" John said, holding his hand up like Geronimo. "Worse than that, do you know whose wallet we just lifted?"

"Yeah, his name is Fletcher Howard, so?"

"Sooo, according to Wharton, he's the Michael Corleone of the Nephilim world. One bad dude."

"No idea who that is," Em said shaking her head, "no idea, but I'll go with it."

"So, out the back we go. We're staying across the street."

They left the Westin through the back lobby entrance and John headed directly towards the train station. They arrived just as the train pulled up. The doors opened to an almost empty car and John took the first available seat. Before Em could join him, he jumped up, grabbed her hand leaving the valise behind and led her back off the train onto the platform. The train's doors closed, and it began to silently move away.

"Great. How do you plan to pay fo-"

John stood grinning, waving the wallet at her. They sat at the empty station discreetly going through the wallet and removed the money and credit cards. He had multiple ids and accompanying documents. John handed the money to Em producing a puzzled look of surprise on her face. John smiled back.

"You trust me?" she said with a raised eyebrow.

"Is there a reason I shouldn't? I mean, are you some sort of double agent working some nefarious plan for your Neph boss? And when I least expect it..." he drew his finger across his throat.

"Well, while we're on the subject of trust..." Em pulled up her pant leg, lowered her sock and produced the manuscript.

"That was in my pocket!" an indignant John replied. "How'd you snatch that?"

"I've been boostin' cars since I was eight. Pickin' pockets isn't rocket science ya' know."

"Really?"

"Did you think it *was* rocket science?" she teased.

"I mean about the cars! Seriously!?" Em could sense John was a bit flustered, but she just couldn't resist. The small person in her derived a little too much pleasure from it.

"Think about it," she said, "I grew up in the jungle. I didn't even *see* a car until I was 17- unless you count the ones Sam made out of bamboo." She laughed. "It's just a girl thing. And I'm nosy."

"What's it say?" John asked.

"Get me wet." she replied. John was speechless. "The manuscript? **SAYS?** she joked. "We need water to read it." Em looked at him sideways, "What did you think I said?"

They headed up the opposite side of the street and John, this time, succeeded in hailing a yellow cab. Em automatically got in.

"Ahh! I forgot my wallet. So sorry. We'll have to go back and get it. Sorry! We'll have to catch another one. Sorry!" Despite John's apologies, the cabbie did a miserable job of hiding his displeasure. John grabbed Em's hand and helped her out of the cab. In the process, he stuffed the wallet deep down in the seat crevice and shut the door.

"Are we ever really going...somewhere?" a frustrated Em asked.

"Sure," John said, holding a fistful of cash. "Right here. Let's check in." They were standing directly in front of the Ritz-Carlton.

"Fancy!" she remarked and then suddenly stopped. "Ohhh! The wallet's headed in the opposite direction." I get it...How'd you learn to be so clever?"

"WWJD." an expressionless John answered.

"What would Jesus do?" John shook his head no.

"What would *Jason* do." Em was confused. John continued, "There isn't a guy alive who doesn't want to be Jason Bourne." Em still didn't put it together. "I went to the movies as a kid- a lot. Umm, it's a guy thing."

John and Em checked in under the name of Darren and Samantha Stevens paying a whopping $850.00 for the room, in cash, in advance by first passing a soggy $100.00 bill to the front desk clerk. Em took the lead and launched into a convincing story how she and Darren fell into some fountain after a bit too much wine tasting where "all their ID and credit cards were lost!" Such a shame. John was torn between concern and outright awe of her ability to spontaneously create the smallest of details as she spun this incredible web of lies. John was also quick to realize the clerk had stopped listening or caring pretty much once the $100 bill had made its way across the marble countertop and began to nudge Em to move it along. As they made their way to the elevator, John wondered how a girl raised in the jungles of Tanna could have developed such street smarts. Sure, there were occasional moments of innocence but for the most part he couldn't help but be impressed by this new, savvy family member. He didn't dare give it breath, but he also couldn't help but think if circumstances were different what a great girlfriend she'd make. Scary good looks, fierce, self-reliant with just a touch of naiveté'- not to mention some really impressive gymnastic fighting skills. If it turned out she knew her way around a video controller and things were different, chances were good he would've proposed to her before the elevator reached the 12th floor.

"1218... to the right" John pointed out. He grabbed Em's backpack and handed her the key card. She opened the door and they both stood on the landing while Em searched for the light switch, but the lights came on automatically. They stood there for a moment, mouths agape, staring at the sunken living room before them. It was cavernous and sumptuously appointed with a huge, king sized bed as it's focal point. They both burst into laughter.

"Holy shit!" John said in disbelief.

"Look at this place!" Em gushed. "Oh my God! Look at that bed!" She wasted no time throwing herself on it, hugging the chamois pillows and rolling back and forth. John looked away nervously.

"Uh, I'm gonna take a quick shower," John announced.

"Me too."

"Oh! Do *you* want to go first?" John asked.

"No."

"Then I should go...Now?" nodding, "Now." John stammered.

"Okee Dokee." she said with a playful grin spreading across her face.

"Okee Dokee? Okee Dokee!?! Geez, she's *enjoying* making me nervous!" he thought. He entered the bathroom, turned the hot water on and tossed the door shut. He began to remove his cold, wet, plaster infused clothing and the heat from the billowing steam felt good against his cold, damp skin. The door never completely latched and unbeknownst to him had opened slightly. Em happened to glance over from her position on the bed and immediately shot upright, her eyes visibly widened. There was John's near flawless form on display wearing nothing but steam clouds. She grimaced in that OMG, finger biting, holy crap fashion and decided to sneak over for a closer look. She grabbed her phone and took a selfie with John's naked, V-shaped back in the steamy background. She quickly reapplied her lipstick, mussed her hair a bit and pulled down on her V neck T-shirt and snapped another.

She scurried over to her backpack and began to dig around inside. With a quick flick of her wrist, a shiny blade snapped into position and she snuck back over to the partially opened bathroom door. If she had been trying to make John nervous before, had he been aware, this move would have guaranteed her success.

She quickly raised her hand over her head and threw the knife across the room. It stuck deep into her intended target, a ripened orange in the fresh fruit bowl arrangement next to the enormous flat screen. She proceeded to cut it into quarters.

From just outside the door, leaning against the adjacent wall she called out to John.

"Hey! want an orange?"

"Yeah. NO! uh... maybe when I get out!"

Em was not waiting and had already begun to sample it. And she did so in X-rated style.

"These are soooo good! Mmmm... you've got to try 'em." John stopped to listen.

"Uh... yeah, I will, yeah."

Em went back to her bag, checking to be sure John wasn't watching and began rummaging around again. This time she produced a large, scary hypodermic needle, the oversized, disposable kind often used by veterinarians to tranquilize animals. She then took a small glass bottle filled with a minute amount of clear liquid and filled the syringe to capacity. She flicked it, testing it to remove any bubbles and began walking towards the steamy shower. With each step, an article of clothing came off so that by the time she reached the shower door she too was completely naked. And completely, stunningly, beautiful.

The steam was so thick as she raised the needle it would have been easy to imagine it being part of a girl-gone-crazy murder mystery, but its target was not John's vulnerable back but rather the remaining pieces of quartered orange. She had used the remaining contents from an old airline bottle of Tito's Vodka she had discovered in the bottom of her bag and was intent on sharing it with John. John's head was under the shower when something touched his shoulder. Em had slipped in and shoved an orange in his mouth from behind.

"Here's that orange with a little something extra." Em bit into a slice as well. "Oh! a lot something extra!" Completely flustered and talking with an orange wedged in his mouth, he tightly shut his eyes and turned to face her.

"Princess Leia! Princess Leia!"

"What?" she asked.

"Princess Leia!" John mush mouthed. Em reached up and pulled the orange out of his mouth. His eyes were still closed. "You know... like in *Star Wars*?"

"Well...Luke, Luke. I am not your father!"

"He actually didn't say it tha-" Oh! what was he doing?! His eyes still pressed shut.

The funny quips and playful banter suddenly ended and for a moment everything in the world stopped, everything was deadly serious. John opened his eyes and lowered his gaze, looking deep within hers. Her hands moved up to his broad shoulders and slowly slid them towards his back. John reached out, placing his hand on her hip, and slid it across her glistening skin coming to rest just above the small of her back. His other hand found its way to her cheek and gently tilted her head upward. She was, in a word, phenomenal. Any line between what was right or wrong, moral, or not was dangerously close to being blurred. This was neither the place nor the circumstances under which he would have chosen to tell her about their connection but felt he no longer had a choice.

"If only things were diff..." John was unable to finish, distracted by Em's sudden change in expression. Em's eyes had been half closed but were now wide open and John felt her body recoil from his. Her hands leaving his back and now covering her mouth. Her eyes no longer locked with his but rather looking behind him, staring steadfast into the floor to ceiling mirror.

"Are you Ok? What is it?" John asked with urgency. Em just continued to stare and point at the mirror. There was genuine fear in her face and John turned to see what it was that struck such abject fear in her.

"No! You! Your back! It's on your back!" She turned him so his back was in the reflection. He struggled to look over his shoulder and what he saw took him aback. There in the steamed-up mirror was a distinct nautilus shape taking up nearly his entire back stretching from shoulder blade to shoulder blade. It was almost scar-like, raised and redder than the surrounding skin. But there was no mistaking it. It wasn't sort of like a nautilus, it was as if someone had carefully drawn its likeness on his skin.

"Game on." John said matter of factly.

"What does it mean?" a concerned Em asked.

"I'm not entirely sure, but I think we're being summoned."

"We? WE!?"

John nodded for her to look in the mirror. She had trouble seeing so John grabbed both her hands and placed them behind her back. She gasped as she felt a small nautilus that had formed just above her tailbone.

"It's Ok," John tried to reassure her. "It's gonna be Ok."

CHAPTER 14

HEEDING THE CALL

Most passengers were asleep including Em. John had been mindlessly leafing through an in-flight magazine wondering why there were so many hair replacement ads. Was that some specific problem unique to male members of the flying public? Just to be sure he reached up and felt the crown of his head. He stopped reading long enough to look at her as she slept. She had that same peaceful look that a rambunctious child has when they finally give in to sleep. He reached over to brush away an errant lock of hair that fell softly across her face. His hand lingered longer than it should, and she stirred, quickly jarring him back to reality. She looked at him and smiled.

"How long was I out? I didn't snore, did I?"

"Nah... just drooled a little '" John teased, pointing to the corner of her mouth.

"Oh! gross!" Em checked herself. "So, there's a trial?"

"Well, kangaroo court. Word is in the village, it's John Frum."

"But there is no John Frum," Em added. "And it's not you, so... who is it?"

"I'm thinking it's the last one the villagers' *thought* was John Frum. And if that's the case..."

Em interrupted. "It could be your father?"

John's eyes locked with hers. He hadn't planned to tell her quite yet but now was as good a time as any. He lowered his head and whispered,

"*Our* father."

Em's eyes closed as she bowed her head. "...who art in heaven, hallowed by thy name. Thy kingdom come, thy will be done, on earth as it is in heaven." She looked up. "I'm sorry, I don't know the rest," she whispered.

"*Ok, maybe not tonight,*" he thought. He had the biggest grin plastered across his face. "You did great," he assured her. "Thank you."

"When I asked Professor Wharton about the whole nautilus thing appearing, I mean it's weird right? I mean, really...otherworldly weird. You don't seem that freaked out. How is-"

"You forget." she interrupted. "I was brought up there. As a little girl I heard stories. I saw things. I saw things growing up that would spin most people's heads. When I left to go to school, simple things in the outside world freaked *me* out. Facetime? Forget it. Witchcraft. But when I would tell people about the things I saw and lived through as a kid, everyone just thought I was making it up, so I learned early on to keep to myself. That's when I realized that western knowledge, as good as it can be, can also blind people to the possibilities found *outside* the senses world."

"As in the five senses. Yeah, yeah, a guy at the Kava ceremony told me about it. And you're right. I'm just starting to wrap my head around it. Wharton says that we're all being summoned by the Elders. Are you familiar...do you even know who the Elders are?"

Em paused and stared at the blue carpeted floor before answering. She nervously played with the edges of the in-flight magazine's worn pages in the seat back pocket.

"If the Elders are really summoning you, this is huge." Em started to cry and quickly turned away. It caught John off guard, and he immediately reached out to console her.

"It's ok. What's wrong?" John asked.

"Sorry," she said, quickly composing herself. "Ugh. um...," she let out a tiny laugh, fanning her face with her hand. "It just makes me a little scared. Because of what...it implies." She undid her seatbelt and turned to face John.

"Only those who have been to the interior have ever seen them." She paused again knowing that he had been sent into the interior and survived. Most did not. She was studying his reaction. "According to legend, they are the true believers that long ago retreated to the interior to remain pure and guide our people through troubling times. Most of the supernatural stuff people talk about are generally due to the Elder's Koontal. Legend has it that there will come a time when the giants will attempt to return to rule the world. Nephilim. There have been increased sightings and incidents lately, which is a sign of what has been foretold- but that marks...," she paused, and her eyes closed in a long, held blink, "the beginning of the end." John was silent, listening.

"Ya know how Christians believe there are certain things to look for, certain signs that indicate that the beginning of the process for the return of Jesus has begun?" John had a blank look on his face.

John grimaced, "Ethan would know. His parents made him go to Sunday school."

"We'll," Em continued, " one major event to watch for is the opening of the East gate of Jerusalem. It's been sealed shut for centuries. Once it's opened, it's said to usher in the beginning of the countdown of the prophecy. The summoning of the Elders of all the true believers is our East gate. And it won't be pretty."

"I don't know if I'm really a, you know, believer, I mean-"

"Doesn't matter," she said, shaking her head. "*They* know." She let that sink in. "The fact that you went in and came out, alive? That should be enough to convince you. But even if you're not now a believer, you will be. It's said that the Elders can peer into the future."

There was a clunk and a rush of air as the landing gear deployed.

"Well, I guess I will find out soon enough," John said, peering out the window. "There's Tanna."

John and Em made their way by outrigger to the shores of the village and trudged the last steamy half mile on foot towards the jungle airstrip.

"Betu ashi! Betu ashi!`` The villagers greeted Em with smiles. The children all rushed to greet her, giggling, and grabbing her hands, touching with curiosity, her jeans, her t-shirt, her hair. The single village men all stopped what they were doing. They all smiled and outstretched their arms in invitation, clutching their heart. It was a markedly different greeting for John. The last time he was here, he was the Messiah, revered by most, looked upon with distrust by a small few but it was always a scene wherever he went. Without his white ash cosmetics, now dressed in jeans, khaki shirt, and sunglasses he was merely a mild curiosity. For the moment he was incognito and that was simply fine with him. Em, however, was clearly the returning celebrity. Everyone knew Emerald. Everyone loved Emerald.

One woman broke through the crowd, quickly approached, hugging her and began frantically speaking to her in Bislama. Em listened. Nodding in understanding she replied to her in Bislama as well. The woman smiled in relief, hugged her again, this time with more intensity and continued on the pathway towards the beach waving until she was out of sight.

"Everything ok?" John asked.

"Oh, yeah. She has six children all under the age of 8 and they got into her grandparent's bones and now she doesn't know whose is whose."

"Wait. Are these bones the grandparents *have*, or is this *THE* Grandparent's...bones?"

"Yeah, this is nana and pappy- or what's left after they've been dried out. Ancestry and lineage are paramount to these folks. I'm just going to put Humpty back together again. No big deal."

"You can do that?"

"Uh huh. That's what I do, sorta, remember?"

Professor Wharton was already there, barking orders in Bislama to his men. The villagers were all dressed in their customary finery for an event of this magnitude.

After all, it was not often that a magistrate came to their little corner of the world. Most had no idea why he had come but welcomed the distraction and wanted to be a part of it.

John looked at Em and said, "I should have known he would beat us here. He didn't say a word when I spoke to him, but come to think of it, he wasn't surprised either when I told him about the nautilus appearing."

Wharton turned in time to see them approaching. His face lit up and his arms opened wide in greeting Em.

"It has been *too* long! How are you sweetness?" Their embrace was warm and long held. "You look great!" the professor said, "I see you've met my worst student."

"Ouch?" John reacted. "Nice to see you too."

"Oh, Professor, I think there's reason to hope. He has a few useful skills," Em said, shooting John a glance.

"Well, no time to waste. The trial is scheduled to start this afternoon and we need to be there." Professor Wharton said as he tied up his pack. "Sam's gone to get us some sort of transportation- otherwise we'll never make it. It's too far to hike it, at least it is for me...now."

Sitting at the far end of the runway near the remains of a dilapidated fueling shed sat a crude version of a Grumman Hellcat fighter. The detail was certainly amazing considering it had been, like everything else, made entirely of bamboo and jungle vines.

"We could just fly there," Professor Wharton joked, pointing towards the Hellcat.

"As long as John's not our pilot," Em was quick to add. John just smiled and shook his head.

Not long after the distant sound of combustion, otherwise foreign to these parts, became increasingly louder, culminating with Sam roaring around the corner of the shed riding a motorcycle. But not just any motorcycle. It was a 1944 Army issue Harley-Davidson complete with a sidecar and from the looks of it, it probably hadn't been disturbed since the day the allies left. Other than being a little dirty and dusty, it was in pristine condition. John suddenly flashed on how his life had so drastically changed in the last few weeks. Seeing an elderly tribal chief, dressed in full ceremonial regalia screaming down a jungle path atop a Harley, while not exactly commonplace, failed to be astonishing. He wasn't sure if life was entirely good, but it surely wasn't boring.

"My ass hurts just looking at that thing," the professor lamented. Sam hobbled off the seat, his near permanent grin pinned on his face.

"Yes. Very fast." he shouted above the idling bike. The professor grimaced.

"Sam, is this the best you can do? I mean-"

"Yes. Very fast." Sam yelled. Turning to John, Professor Wharton asked,

"You know anything about these things?"

"How hard can it be?" John quipped. The professor and Em began loading their things into the bike's limited storage space.

Sam limped over to John. His smile was now gone.

"We call and you came. God Bless America John Frum. They take Heylia. Giants take her, John Frum."

"What!?"

"Four giants hold me." Sam began to weep. "Take her away. To inside." He quickly collected himself.

"You will find her, John Frum. You remember your time inside with elders. You be...John Frum."

John was left reeling at the news of Heylia's kidnapping. Everything went white. He stood paralyzed for a moment, unable to speak. This could not be possible. It could *not* be possible. This was little Heylia. She was ten years old for Christ's sake! He knew all too well her fate if he didn't act quickly. With new found conviction, he looked at Sam intently, reached out and held his shoulders,

"I will try."

Sam abruptly recoiled, moving back in disbelief and shook his head. "No try!" No try! There is no try, only do!"

John's eyes narrowed, studying Sam's face. Did he just quote Yoda? Slowly a mischievous smile crept onto Sam's face. He leaned in now grabbing John's shoulders and slowly whispered,

"You Tube. You find her John Frum! You bring her back to me!" He turned and walked away leaving John perplexed and stunned.

CHAPTER 15

HEADING TO THE KANGAROO COURT

Harleys were never known for their quiet, subtle idle. It was loud and commanding in 1944 and time did nothing to diminish that. John reverted to hand signals, hopped aboard, motioned to Em who slithered in behind him leaving the professor to squeeze his less than svelte body into the sidecar. He grimaced as he endeavored to find *any* position that might offer the slightest comfort. Bucking and snorting, they made their way noisily down the dirt trail that would eventually lead to the old meeting house where the trial was to be held.

Not long into their ride they rounded a wide corner and came upon a small group of howler monkeys congregating in the middle of the trail. John slowed as he completed the turn, inadvertently squaring off as they all stopped and stared. Even John knew, in his limited experience, one or two were cute-mischievous, but cute. A group like this, however, could be serious trouble and their sudden presence along with the blatting Harley had clearly agitated them. John immediately shut the bike down. As he looked around, he realized the howlers that were in front of him were merely the tip of an extraordinarily large primate iceberg. He cautiously glanced up into the surrounding trees and saw hundreds of reinforcements, their mouths agape, their eyes blinking, waiting, watching for a signal to join the party. This was not good. Not good at all. Professor was the first to speak, albeit quietly.

"Everybody easy."

"This is one group you do not want to piss off," Em whispered.

"Ok. We're all going to get off. Very slowly," he added. "Don't face them directly, don't look into their eyes. No smiles- especially smiles with teeth. Now, try to look as big and as bad as you possibly can... slowly!"

They began puffing themselves up, blowing out their cheeks and standing on tiptoes with arms and fingers outstretched. Pretty much looking ridiculous, actually. And it soon became clear it wasn't really working- at all. The obvious leader began slowly advancing, testing their resolve, challenging the group.

John, Em, and the professor were standing with eyes straight ahead, motionless, doing their best to talk without moving their mouths.

"Watch this grey one." John whispered. "He's the loudest one of the bunch,"

"They can get up to 128 decibels," Em, always at the ready with the facts, informed them. "A jet engine gives off 140. But never mind the grey. He's got the smallest testicles... and the rest of them know it."

"What?" John whisper shouted.

"Studies show that the ones with the smallest testicles are the loudest. They compensate for the lack of... well you know...by howling the loudest. Keep your eye on the big red one. He's the boss."

"Kind of like guys in a bar," quipped Professor Wharton.

It wasn't that funny, perhaps it was the nervousness wrought by the situation, but it caught John off guard, and he let out a loud, open mouth guffaw. Teeth and all. Professor Wharton's head cocked back, and his eyes rolled skyward in disbelief. This did not sit well with the howlers. The grey was the first to register his displeasure. He began hooting and howling, slapping the ground with his open palms, thrashing, and throwing dust in the air. For the recruits in the trees, this was the bugler's call, the playing of charge and down they came, descending from every tree within a half mile. There were now at least a hundred of them gathered, the sound, terrifying.

Then out of the growing dust cloud, came Big Red, doing that sideways gallop that monkeys do, wild-eyed and baring his four, very sharp, front fangs. Em was right. This *was* the ringleader and he and his monstrous testicles were racing straight towards them.

Suddenly and without warning, a cannon-like boom rang out. Instinctively, John and the professor cowered, grabbing their ears, lowering their heads. Standing between them stood Em. One hand placed on her hip the other holding a chrome and pearl handled 357 Magnum over her head, a small wisp of smoke now trailing from the elongated barrel as she slowly lowered her arm. John and Professor Wharton were stunned, as well as nearly deaf.

"What in holy hell was that!?" screamed John.

"Whoa! Keep your voice down! People will think you have... you know," she smirked, holding two fingers close together.

John rolled his eyes and demanded in a whisper, "What was that!?"

"American diplomacy. C'mon, we're wasting time."

The howlers dispersed quicker than a school of fish startled by a hungry shark, but the ringleader remained. Em could see he was contemplating a second attempt. She turned, squared off and raised her gleaming hand cannon in his direction, putting him directly in her sights. She cocked the hammer back and it made that unmistakable sound of deadly intent.

"Unless you want to be the loudest howler in the bunch, don't. Just don't." she yelled.

On some primal level it was as if Big Red somehow knew she had both the skill set and the resolve to pull it off. So, with one final, defiant howl, he reluctantly and wisely turned away, slipping into the shadows of the bush.

John straddled the knucklehead and stood on the kickstarter, but it failed to ignite. There was a certain amount of urgency tied to getting this thing lit and on their way. There was a genuine concern that the howlers might regroup and decide to make a second go at it. Unless Em was hiding a surprise rocket launcher in her backpack (which, he guessed, was now a possibility) her 357 only held six shots and one was already gone. Maybe the howlers were smart enough and willing to sacrifice five of their group so that the others could have an amazing lunch. He just didn't know and wasn't keen on hanging around to find out. And there was the trial. It was going to happen with or without them and without transportation, they'd never make it in time. He tried it again. And again. And again. He tried so many times he was now sweating and winded, but it didn't even hint at starting.

"Hold on before you all mount up," John said as he checked the ignition. It was on. Choke was fine. He unscrewed the gas cap and peered down into the tank, but it was dark. He gave it a rap with his knuckles, and it sounded curiously empty, which was odd- they hadn't gone that far. He shot a worried glance towards the professor and used his phone's flashlight to get a good look inside. What he saw took him aback. Not only was it empty, but it was also bone-dry. Like rusted, dead leaves and cobwebs bone-dry. He cleared the top of the tank of the sticky cobwebs and once again looked down into the dry, rusted tank. John was utterly baffled. Professor Wharton was now laughing and laughing hard.

"But we *RODE* here!" John protested, trying to make sense of what he saw in the tank.

"Sam!" Professor Wharton could hardly get it out; he was now laughing so hard. "Sam... Koontal," he managed to say, shaking his head. "Of course..."

John just stood staring down into the empty tank.

"Ya' know what you're looking at?" asked Professor Wharton.

"Yeah. Yeah, an empty tank."

"Look again."

"What!? I'm looking! What am I looking at!?"

After a long pause Professor Wharton, suddenly serious, sighed and turned, looking directly at John.

"Doubt." he said while slowly nodding, "You're looking at doubt."

The professor turned and began gathering his things readying himself for the long walk ahead.

John's face said it all. He stared at the ground, motionless, wearing the face of someone who was summoning every ounce of restraint, for fear his frustration would gush out of every pore in a raging torrent.

Em had joined the professor and they began walking down the trail. Professor Wharton, seemingly much more able to take it in stride, was still grinning. He licked his finger and swiped across his palm pretending to turn the pages of an imaginary book.

"If you should say unto this mountain, be thou removed and cast into the sea... *and do not doubt*," he bellowed, emphasizing with an upheld hand, "It shall be done unto them!"

"Well, what chapter and verse of Darwin's writings did *that* come from?" John shouted back in anger.

John looked at the bike, then at them and back to the lifeless bike again. He let out a sigh as his chin fell to his chest in apparent defeat. Professor Wharton cast a reassuring smile towards Em who seemed concerned for John.

"He'll be fine, just give him some time. I should have known Sam would have...well, you remember from growing up how many times Sam would use Koontal to-"

Suddenly the sound of the Harley roaring to life stopped them dead in their tracks. Em and the professor remained perfectly still. Their eyes as big as saucers like an anxious couple on a midnight stroll through a dark cemetery, listening intently to confirm the sound of a snapping twig behind them. John rolled up on them, a small dust cloud accompanying him and stared straight ahead. He continued staring straight ahead and all three remained wordless. After a very long pause,

"OK," he said, his head still nodding slightly, " OK... I get it."

THE TRIAL

The meeting house where the trial was to be held was once home to a long-ago English missionary's church. Time had healed most of the bad memories associated with it. Most, but not all and any stranger was always received with a bit of wariness because of it. It seems around the turn of the century a small group of white, uninvited religious zealots arrived with the intention of civilizing the heathens and improving their lives. In short order, they banned the drinking of Kava, referring to it as 'the devils brew' and had the children convinced their nakedness was bad, dressing them in traditional English whites, pants, and ties. They were made to attend church services where they would learn the error of their ways and how much better off they would be once the social graces of English culture and religion had been fully absorbed. They even had them take part in a daily high tea. Nothing says 'civilized' like an afternoon tea and cucumber finger sandwiches. The villagers endured this poppycock for an entire 6 months before reciprocating with a Kava infused tea of their own and then sending the intoxicated group off to the interior. They never did reappear, and the children were quickly relieved of their uniforms and returned to their unholy nakedness. The village recycled the clothing into many useful things, one of which was the huge American flag that gets dragged out every February 15th in celebration of Tanna USA Day.

The old church was put to good use as well. It was now used for anything that required large numbers of the community to assemble, such as weddings or official council meetings. There were rows of hard, wooden benches that the newly converted would sit on while being subjected to the daily fire and brimstone sermons. Those benches, adorned with native carvings and paintings were now filled with the curious, not sure what they were going to see, but the arrival of a Magistrate was a rare event indeed and few wanted to miss it. It was almost a party-like atmosphere except for the few, ridiculously tall men peppered throughout the hall that sat stoically, staring straight ahead.

"You people should have a basketball team- Look at the size of them...what tribe are they from?" The Magistrate's question went unanswered.

There was a nervousness in the air as the native volunteers set about the tasks of readying the venue. The Magistrate, a balding, pasty white porker of a man and his nerdy, bespeckled bookworm clerk were in the back room behind a raised stage, separated from the noisy crowd only by a thin, tattered, makeshift curtain. There were a number of religious artifacts, remnants of that misguided mission that were strewn about and piled in leftover wooden ammo boxes. A small table with a galvanized metal wash basin sat in the center of the stuffy backroom.

"Crimony! It's so bloody hot. How *do* you people stand it?" the Magistrate said to no one in particular as he began donning his black robe. "So, who is this miserable old sot anyway?"

"The villagers say he's John Frum, your honor," The magistrate turned and looked at his clerk over the top of his thin rimmed glasses. "Yes," the clerk affirmed, "*that* John Frum." The Magistrate cynically smiled.

"And what is he being accused of?"

A voice rang out from the doorway, "He has willfully misled my people for years claiming to be the returning messiah, John Frum!"

"I'm sorry, who are you?" an indignant Magistrate inquired.

"Fletcher Howard your honor and my people wish-"

"My people? My people!? Good God man! Have you looked in a mirror? You're a couple of shades off from these savages. And why is this so suddenly important? So bloody important as to pull me away from the Cricket World Cup to come to this God-forsaken jungle?"

Fletcher Howard shot a look at some of the villagers and almost as if on cue they took up his argument. One extremely tall villager stepped forward and in broken English spoke to the Magistrate.

"He bad. He bad for people. He promise to...."

The Magistrate had already lost interest and was now peering out from the curtain towards the unruly, boisterous crowd. There sat the accused, surrounded by his accusers who were busy taunting, poking, and prodding him. He abruptly shushed the villager and spoke to his clerk while observing the escalating tension in the now packed house.

"Sure, doesn't look very Messiah-like to me. Has he hurt anyone? Physically? I mean, is he dangerous?"

"No, your honor."

"Is he of the Crown?" He was clearly worried by what he saw brewing amongst the ever-swelling crowd.

"No, your honor, he's American. We think."

"American!? American??"

He began washing his hands in the basin, continuing to look at his clerk in disbelief.

"American. This is *clearly* not our affair!" He looked about to see who would bring him a towel. There was no one. "These savages want his hide... far be it from us to meddle in local affairs. Yet here we are... Alright," he said in exasperation, "let's get on with it."

The clerk went out first arranging the seat behind the crude desk where he draped a banner across its front. It was impressive- A golden threaded Coat of Arms against a dark blue satin background, the Seal of the Queen on one side and a British flag on the other. Three distinct raps of his gavel and the trial was under way.

John, Em, and the professor had just arrived, ditching the bike before the last half mile so as to not draw attention to themselves. The crowd had grown so large there were about a hundred onlookers assembled just outside the open doors and the trio slipped into their midst making their way through the sea

of sweaty bodies towards the front. From there they could see the Magistrate taking his seat on the stage.

"Your attention please! Order! Order in the court! The honorable Lord Viceroy, Queen's Magistrate presiding. On this day of our Lord..."

"Yes! Yes!" interrupted the Magistrate, "that's enough...that's fine." he said waving his hand. "Moving on..."

"Please be seated." Even though no one had risen, "The people's representative will now present their case," the clerk announced in a loud voice. Fletcher Howard rose, standing next to the cloaked defendant, clearing his throat to address the court.

"Your honor, some 26 years ago this man led a group of so-called scientists who came to this pristine jungle with the intent of corrupting a pure and otherwise untainted society for monetary gain at the expense of-"

Suddenly the accused rose, interrupting the proceedings. He was dressed in sackcloth, a large hood obscuring his identity yet spoke in a commanding voice.

"It is you who has handed over the keys of hell to these evil, hybrid half-humans. It is you who is the whited sepulcher, holding nothing but death and destruction as a future for these good people, the tribes of Tanna! You, Mr. Howard and your ilk, are a stench in the very nostrils of God!"

An enraged Fletcher Howard suddenly slapped the prisoner with such force as to cause his hood that had hidden his identity to fall away. It revealed a defiant Aiden, and the crowd began to move towards him. John was shocked and confused. He doubted that it would truly turn out to be his father but never in a million years did he expect to see Aiden.

"He's been set up!" shouted John. Professor Wharton, now frantic, looked at John and exclaimed,

"No. We've been!"

"We don't need to hear anymore!" screamed one of the taller members. He stood, revealing his 7+ feet tall frame and began to make his way towards Aiden.

"Kill him!"

"Order! Order!" the magistrates gavel repeatedly slammed down on the wooden desk. The giant stopped his advance and quickly turned towards the bench.

"This is our concern!" he said, pointing a threatening finger towards the Magistrate. Em was the first to notice his extended, pointing finger was one of six on his left hand. He addressed the crowd, "Do we want judgement on this white devil being decided by another white man?"

The crowd exploded in choruses of "No! Kill the white devil!" Kill him!" and quickly rose to their feet. This was the excuse the masses were looking for and the giants among them seized the moment and began fomenting the crowd. It quickly escalated to full blown chaos with benches being thrown and fists flying. The courageous Magistrate and his brave sidekick quietly slipped out the back and disappeared into the shadowy jungle. John instinctively turned to run to the aid of his friend when Professor Wharton grabbed him by the shoulders. He forcefully turned him and looked him dead in the eyes.

"We are the target! Understand?! I can't do this without you. Stand with me, hand on my shoulder. Clear your mind. NO DOUBT!" he shouted.

"No doubt." John parroted.

Professor Wharton took a deep breath, closed his eyes, and exhaled. John, for the first time followed his lead without question and did the same thing. He thought it odd that the professor, in times of great need, did exactly what he had always done since he was a kid. But now was no time to question or wonder. He cleared his mind, closed his eyes, and let out his own singular, exhaling breath and in so doing, **TIME STOPPED.**

That is, for everyone except Professor Wharton. John reopened his eyes. He was unaware of any passage or interruption of time, the same way that in sleep, hours can pass by yet upon waking, seems instantaneous. Somehow Wharton was now on the opposite side of him, wearing a totally inappropriate half smile on his face. The brutal beating was in the process of being carried out, leaving John horrified until the crowd, having finished its work, stopped, and pulled back the sackcloth hood. It was a bloodied and beaten Fletcher Howard barely conscious and near death, choking on his own blood. The crowd grew quickly silent, confused by Fletcher's sudden appearance in the accused's tattered robe.

"Em, take your father to the airfield. We'll meet up there." said the professor. Em and Aiden were already at the very back of the rowdy crowd leaning against an old beater Jeep pick-up. It was missing its hood among other things but had the keys in the ignition so, hey... finders-keepers. She helped Aiden into the back of the open-air Jeep.

"Aiden is her *dad*!?" John asked in complete surprise.

"Well, yeah. Thought you knew that," said the professor. "Thought you'd be a little more impressed with the other thing..." John wore a clueless expression. " You know, the whole...little...time-altering switcheroo...thing? Look, Aiden probably wasn't the best choice, but he stepped up when Em's parents disappeared."

Fletcher Howard's henchmen had suddenly noticed John and the Professor and that their truck was being commandeered.

"Time to go!" The professor and John ran towards Aiden and Em and threw themselves into the truck. Em floored it, spinning the bald tires, throwing pebbles and dirt back at their pursuers. Fishtailing as they went, she headed down the dusty trail and into the security of the enveloping jungle.

As the jungle swallowed them up and they began to put some distance between themselves and the mayhem left behind, the group silently began to gather themselves. What had they all just witnessed? That brief respite was short lived however, shattered by a tremendous crashing sound that came from behind causing them all to turn in unison. There was a flurry of activity in the brush behind them as leafy branches began to be yanked down out of nowhere and disappear.

Then, out of the broken branches and in a great storm of dirt and leaves appeared a monstrously huge Nephilim. Human but not, with animal-like actions coupled with disproportionately large human features. The brain actually had trouble reconciling the distorted image it saw. But the one thing the brain had no trouble with, was alerting the adrenaline producers of the body to start firing on all cylinders. Make no mistake, he was coming for them and with great speed, sometimes literally galloping on all fours, snarling like a rabid, junkyard dog. Except this junkyard dog was off his chain and would not be distracted.

"Must go faster!" Aiden blurted out.

"I can't get it out of second!" Em yelled as she continued forcefully pushing on the floor shifter. John joined the effort to move the shifter into third but to no avail. He looked around for something with a bit of weight to it to pound the shifter forward but only came up with a can of starter fluid that had rolled out from under his seat. It did, however, give him an idea. He rolled out the open side window, steadied himself with one hand by grabbing onto the window pillar, reached over to the exposed air cleaner and began loosening it's wing nut. Just as he removed the air cleaner's lid, he glanced back. The Neph was now a mere foot away from the Jeep's tailgate, his hand outstretched, poised to grab Aiden's flapping shirt tail.

"Behind you!" John yelled. Without a thought, John frisbeed the lid towards the giant, catching him squarely on the bridge of his oversized nose. It watered his eyes just enough to cause him to stumble. As they sped away the dust cloud cleared enough to see him crumpled in a heap off to the side of the trail. The unspoken "Geez, that was close" sentiment shared by all was apparent. The nervous smiles of relief however were quickly wiped away when the determined Neph came crashing back out of the jungle. He was back in the race and quickly gaining on them.

"Still. Can't. Get. Third!!" Em shouted, struggling with the gearshift.

"Bloody move!!" screamed Aiden. He raised his boot and kicked the stick shift forward, grinding it into third. At the same time John aimed the can of starter fluid and sprayed the liquid horsepower directly into the open carburetor causing the fully taxed engine to suddenly howl with renewed life and the Jeep flew forward.

The defeated giant filled Em's side mirror, standing upright in the middle of the trail having finally given up the race. He was at least twelve feet tall. "Where had he come from?" she thought. Up until now, the only twelve footers were the ancient dead ones found in her archaeological digs. This was new. This was troubling. They were running out of time.

The rest of the journey was spent not speaking. Everyone was in some sort of post prize fight daze, trying to process the events of the last few days. So, little of it was...normal. The sneaking suspicion was that abnormality was about to become the norm and no one was keen on embracing it.

The Jeep squealed to a halt on the dusty airstrip just yards from the rusting hanger. In it was Aiden's little BackCountry Super Cub, a bush plane replete with those funny looking fat balloon tires for landing pretty much anywhere. It always made John smile when he saw it because to him it looked like one of those Pixar cartoon characters, like a little kid wearing dad's big shoes. It was mustard yellow with red markings and had the look of something salvaged from a defunct McDonalds franchise. Its beauty was in its simplicity which consequently was the reason for its reliability. There just weren't enough extra bells and whistles to break down and go wrong. An engine, a wing, a seat, and a stick to steer it. What else did one need?

John helped Aiden load the plane with supplies- enough to carry him for a few days.

"Aiden, I'm going to need you to pick up Ethan and the guys. Oh man! Wait wait, that's a nasty cut above your eye!" John reached out and cradled his head to get a better look. Aiden pushed him away.

"It's just a bloody scratch! That's the problem- you're too soft. You've led a comfy life. A little scuffle every now and then would've been good for you."

"Well, I'm making up for it now, aren't I?"

"Yeah," he had to admit, "and the one comin' is nothin' to sneeze at."

"And by that you mean the little scuffle that, in all likelihood, will alter the course of human history and determine the future of all mankind, right?

"Something like that, yeah."

John fished around in the beat up first aid kit he'd pulled from the Super Cub and came up with a half-opened butterfly bandage. He continued to look for something a tad cleaner.

"So, you're gonna go to Vanuatu and pick the guys up. Jay's dad has a plane just sitting there- a real plane. You know, one that can fit more than just one ornery old Brit and his fifth of Jack?"

"I had a real plane. Then some wet-behind-the-ears hooligan parked it upside down atop a tree. Atop a tree... who does that!? Can you believe that?" Aiden said with a scowl. John immediately returned fire.

"Oh go, go ahead. Go with Satan's little midget pilot, it'll be fun he said,"

"Touché'," Aiden said matter of factly. "And what if they don't want to leave?"

"You mean the guys? Just tell them that the viral video is back on and that the throngs of naked island girls can't wait to meet them. Just keep your ears on, I've got the two-way hand-held."

He grabbed Aiden by the back of his neck, pulled him in and began blotting the blood from his forehead with his own sleeve. He tore open the butterfly with his teeth and stretched it across Aiden's formidable gash.

"So... all that talk over the years about that one special girl, the one and only you ever truly loved...the one who held the keys to your heart that no other could unlock- was *literally* a little girl."

Aiden nodded and smiled. "She's the only reason I got left." His eyes pooled, drifting off to the side. They returned to look directly into John's. "I'd crawl through crushed glass for little Em, mate."

"Why didn't you tell me?" John asked.

"There were a lot of things I didn't tell you. The less you knew the less danger you'd be in."

Em suddenly walked in.

"There!" John announced, quickly returning to dressing Aiden's wound, " and perfectly sanitary."

"So, Em, I'm going to need you to convince the villagers to do some gardening- a really, really deep garden at the edge of the clearing." Em's face was a question mark. "Can you do that?" He walked over to a workbench. "Here, I'll do a quick sketch of what I'm talking about," John told her. He set about drawing out a rough plan on the back of an old calendar. Professor Wharton had joined them in the hangar.

"Do I smell a plan?"

"Yep. C'mon, I'll explain on the way."

They gathered up their things, bid Aiden goodbye, loaded up the Jeep and the three of them headed for the village center.

CHAPTER 16

A ROUGH WAY TO PROVE YOUR MANHOOD

John made his way towards the leaping tower. There was a Bislamic word for it, the first one being 'jamjam', but the second was too difficult to pronounce, so leaping tower it was. His first experience at the tower didn't go well. When he was first pulled from the wreckage and during his recovery, some of the men, wary of his intentions, goaded him into attempting a leap. Kwanteef, the current reigning champion, was especially skeptical of John and spearheaded the challenge.

Halfway up the tower he nearly passed out just from the rigors of the climb. Realizing his body was nowhere near the condition it needed to be in to be successful, he "chickened out" and had to climb down. It's one thing for a 14-year-old boy to fail but completely another for a grown man to do so. Rarely did men from the tribe 'chicken out' but for the few who did, they were ridiculed and labeled for life. Or at least until they redeemed themselves by successfully jumping from the highest platform.

Constructed over 100 years ago of bamboo and vines and nearly 200 ft high, it rose well above the tallest trees and could be seen from pretty much anywhere. In the aftermath of the allied force's sudden exodus, the tower served as a lookout station for the returning ancestral cargo planes. It was quite rudimentary engineering and design. Four posts, wider at the base than it was at the top with a ladder tied to the outside of its southernmost leg. Small platforms that served as both rest stations and mid-level launching pads were scattered throughout its towering height and at any given time, men could be seen languishing in the breeze on them. At its base was a six-inch layer of palm fronds and leaves, placed there as a safety cushion should the vine fail. It would by no means prevent one's death in the event of a vine failure but at least there was a chance that you'd be recognizable, and your minimal clothing wouldn't get as dirty in the process.

It was a gathering place mostly. For the men of the village, it had great importance in their lives. It was a place where the young men and boys could prove their bravery and secure their social status in the tribe. Diving headfirst off a 200-foot tower with only two spindly vines tied to your ankles preventing your death was a sure-fire way to impress the ladies. And in any culture, it almost always boils down to that.

The men would first go into the jungle in search of a suitable pair of vines. There were strict guidelines for choosing a vine. They had to be the right thickness and length and it had to be the right time of year. The vines needed to have the right moisture content, typically newly grown but not so new as to be susceptible to excessive stretching. Or worse, too old, and too dry causing them to break. Ouch. Those guidelines were broken only once. In February of 1952, a group of visiting British Royals, hoping to witness this bizarre, daring feat were disappointed to learn there would be no leaps as it was past season for the vines. They pressured the tribe to perform the ritual anyway. A young, enthusiastic man was convinced by their paltry offer of a gold-tone Zippo lighter with a Union Jack on its face to leap from the tower using vines that were past their prime and they subsequently snapped. He died of his injuries 3 days later and was buried with his much-coveted Zippo clenched in his fist. There had been no love lost for the British ever since.

"I wish to speak with Kwanteef!" yelled John up to the group of men gathered midway up the tower. Kwanteef appeared from the group, stood at the edge, and peered down at him.

"What does the lady wish to say?" The group laughed. John looked around nodding, smiling knowingly.

"Ok, ok...alright," John conceded.

"In just two days, a great evil will visit upon this land. It will come in the form of men. But not just any men, giant men. Ghost Giants." The snickering stopped; the men grew silent. They knew the term; it was their term and brought with it painful memories. "The Ghost Giants that took your sisters, your mothers, your wives. They're coming to finish the job." John paused and scanned the crowd. "They're coming for you. And you. And you." The look on their faces was a mixture of fear and anger. They knew he spoke the truth. It was the prophecy that had been passed down by the great storytellers of the tribe for generations.

"What makes you so sure?" asked Kwanteef.

"I've been to the interior. And I came back." He paused to let that sink in. No one in recent history had ever come back. "I've seen the scrolls, read the prophecy-

"Why we trust you?" Kwanteef fired at John.

"We can get your women back; we can defeat them! But I need your help..."

"Come back when you be man enough to defeat tower, to defeat me! Then... we talk." With that Kwanteef turned and rejoined his group.

"Stay there! Don't go anywhere," John barked at him.

He turned and walked into the jungle. In no time he returned walking out of the bush. Wrapped around his shoulders and neck was a nest of green vines looking a lot like the jumbled mess of Christmas lights that his uncle would pull down from the attic every December. He strode over to the southernmost leg of the tower and began to climb the ladder. Kwanteef reappeared at the edge peering down as John took some of the rungs two at a time.

"Ful", he pronounced. "Ful! vines not season, he said, shaking his head.

"Fool? Perhaps... but we don't have any time." John said as he reached over and pulled himself onto the top where Kwanteef stood. He sat and tied each vine to his ankle, straining to make them as tight as possible.

"Tie me off? John said as he handed him the ends of his vines. Kwanteef stood frozen staring at John. This was no small gesture. In tribal culture, John was effectively entrusting his life to him.

"You want Kwanteef tie you? Kwanteef," he said, tapping his own chest with his fist.

John kneeled, vines in hand, his arms extended, eyes locked with his. Kwanteef broke his long-held stare to look at the vines, then back at John. He cocked his head to one side, reached across his chest and in one sweeping and startling motion, sliced through the two vines with his massive machete. An astonished John was left holding two three-foot lengths of new vine in his hands.

"Out season vine stretch. Not good. You smoosh ground." Kwanteef turned and took to the task of tying the vines onto a six-inch-thick bamboo support pole. Once satisfied, he turned to face John. John was standing on the very edge, his back to the distant horizon. Kwanteef reached into one of his many pockets and produced a small, worn American flag bandana. He tied it about John's forehead. "*Easy Rider*" he thought.

By this point a crowd had gathered below. Word had quickly spread into the village that the crazy messiah was about to plunge to his death, and few wanted to miss that.

"God Bless America," Kwanteef muttered. He gave John the slightest head nod of confirmation. John took a deep breath, closed his eyes, and gently let the air escape his lungs. Then, just like that, with arms fully extended, his palms facing forward, John allowed himself to fall backwards off the edge and into the warm, tropical sky.

There was an audible gasp from the group below when John's body left the top of the tower. With arms outstretched, the symbolism of a toppling cross was not lost on them. Afterall, for some, this was their Messiah. But halfway down his arms changed position. Unlike an Olympic diver whose hands would've been clasped above his head, they were pressed against his sides, rigid fingers pointing to his feet, literally diving headfirst into danger. For John it seemed like an eternity before he heard the thwack of the slack playing out as the vine reached its full length. He had underestimated just how jarring it would be to go from 143 miles an hour to a complete brick wall stop. It felt as if his entire skeletal structure was attempting to exit his body through his eyes. He hung there motionless, hands and arms still pressed to his sides with his eyes tightly shut. He feared that opening them would cause his eyeballs to fall out and roll away like two grapes on a kitchen counter. Kwanteef placed his hands and the soles of his feet on the outside edge of the ladder and slid down its entire length at near free fall speed. He ran over to John, genuine concern on his face.

"How you, ful?"

A single leaf had stuck to John's nose. He opened his eyes and blew the leaf off. He managed a half smile.

"Alive," he groaned. "Get me down from here."

It was a success. In more ways than John knew. First, he survived… there's that. But the jump itself was unique to say the least. Most tribal members had witnessed hundreds of jumps over the years. The eerie silence of the dive itself followed by the sudden snap made when the vine reaches its limit and then perhaps the most violent part, the erratic swinging of the body like a discarded rag doll until gravity slowed it to a stop. John's dive was no different except in its ending. There was the eerie silence, the snap of a taut vine but absolutely no swinging. No recoil. None. Just a laws-of-physics-defying motionless end to his brief, fool-hardy journey leaving him suspended as if by a steel pole rather than a flexible jungle rope. The crowd was awestruck if not downright frightened at this miraculous sight. The moment of truth had arrived.

"Alright," he paused. "Who's with me?" Dead silence. John looked about. Nothing but wide-eyed, gaped-mouthed dark faces.... blankly staring. "Well if this doesn't do it," he thought, "then noth-"

"AAAAAAAAHHHHH!!!" The tribe erupted in a hellacious roar of approval, chanting, screaming, rushing towards him, raising John up above their shoulders like some high school QB who just threw an 85-yard game winning touchdown. They ran with him atop their shoulders back into the village and were joined by hundreds of others. The sound was deafening. John had his defensive force.

Professor Wharton came out to see what all the ruckus was about. The village immediately cleared the dusty center and began stacking wood in the huge fire pit. There was going to be a pep rally like no other. John dismounted his moving mosh pit and made his way through the throng to where the professor stood.

"Nice work," Professor Wharton said with a smile. "Even got Kwanteef to come along- wow. Impressive! Used your persuasive personality I gather?"

"Uh...something like that... I know where my mother is," John said seemingly out of nowhere. Professor Wharton eyed him intently and with a measure of uncertainty. That was the great thing about him. He never discounted or derided him out of hand. He almost always allowed him to speak out. And then he discounted and derided him.

"How do you know?" he said.

"She gave me this." John reached into his shirt and pulled out the small satchel filled with tiny nautilus shells he had been wearing that

hung from a leather strap around his neck "when I was...you know...
in there."

Professor Wharton stifled a small gasp and reached out to touch
them. The professor's eyes immediately welled up; his mouth partially
open yet unable to speak.

"So, I'm gonna go get her. And I need you to be waiting for us."

Professor Wharton quickly gathered himself and asked, "But you
don't know how long you'll be in there. This whole party is set to start
pretty soon."

"You're right. But for you? It'll be pretty much right after I go in."

"True," conceded the Professor. "But things change in there. You
could lose your way," he cautioned.

"You can lose your way in life too, but you know, eventually you
find a way. Sometimes ya' just gotta risk it." John countered.

"Well, since we're talking about risk...Before you go, why don't you
tell Em how you feel?" John's face went white.

"Whadda you mean? How do I feel about what?"

Professor Wharton scowled a bit. "I've seen how you look at her—
how she looks at you."

John felt as if he had just been caught red handed doing...
something. Something he shouldn't. Something seedy. Up until this
point he genuinely believed his secret was safe and that he had done
a remarkable job of masking any and all of his feelings, not only from
her and the others, but from himself as well. And now it was like his
subconscious had had one too many, and his inner voice was drunk
texting his deepest, darkest thoughts to his entire contacts list for
everyone to see. He was genuinely perplexed as to what to say or do
next.

"Look, I'm old but I'm not dead," Wharton assured him. "Tell her!"

John was confused. "She's...my sister!" he said in hushed tones. "I think."

Professor Wharton laughed. Shaking his head, he laughed so hard he hung his head and reached out to support himself against a nearby tree.

"Not hardly! Whatever gave you that idea?"

"The picture, all that stuff you gave me... she had to be.... Not my sister?"

Professor Wharton was still laughing and shaking his head no.

"Not sister. No. Not...." he couldn't continue. Shaking his head in disbelief, he turned and began walking away. "TELL HER!!" He yelled over his shoulder, still chuckling as he made his way towards the office.

Em had just finished up helping sort out a problem between a mother and a daughter, as she was known to do, had gathered up her stuff and began down the trail towards her hut. As she rounded the corner, John caught a glimpse of her long dark hair through the trees and went straight away to her. He caught up to her, grabbed her by the arm and spun her around, causing her backpack to fall to the ground. He looked deep into her eyes, lowered his head,

"You're not my sister."

He pulled her in by the small of her back, placed his hand gently on her cheek and deep kissed her. He held it until her body went limp, her arms fell to her sides and she was left quietly gasping for air. John turned and began to walk away, leaving her breathless. She shook her head.

"About damn time!" she said.

John turned back just in time to catch her as she jumped up to him, wrapped her tanned legs around his waist and planted a deep kiss of her own squarely on his mouth. It was a long held, passionate embrace of pent up chemistry. As they broke, her hand reached up and caressed his cheek. Staring into one another's eyes, they were breathing each other's breath, their lips barely touching.

"I... I gotta go," he said.

"Mmmm....me too."

CHAPTER 17

SECOND TIME'S THE CHARM

John found his way back to the place where he first entered the interior. He had forgotten how much it had reminded him of Stonehenge and shook his head just as he had when he first saw it in disbelief of finding such an iconic structure in the middle of the South Pacific. He paused trying to remember the exact spot he was standing in when he disappeared. The vegetation had grown so fast that it was hard to pinpoint it. He was trying to recreate in his mind the exact circumstances under which he was whisked away. It dawned on him that he was not entirely sure just how this whole thing worked. Was the tribes' presence required to succeed? Was that weird hissing sound the tribe made some sort of critical component in gaining access? Did they have anything to do with it at all? And there was the Kava. The Kava! He hadn't brought any with him. All these questions began creating a bit of angst in him but then just as quickly remembered what Sam had told him.

"You no need Kava," he mouthed the words as he remembered. He even went so far as to tap his own forehead just as Sam had done to him. "Your Kava here." A wave of peaceful tranquility washed over him. His believing would carry him through, just as it always had. It had to. John closed his eyes, centered himself with a deep, cleansing breath and exhaled. Suddenly he was gone.

He stood motionless and abruptly opened his eyes. They darted side to side without moving a muscle at first. Slowly raising his head up, he began to look around. It was the exact same spot he had arrived at during his first visit, but he was noticeably calmer this time. The first time he didn't know what to expect, everything was new. Now things were a bit more familiar.

At first glance it was a place that was no different than the jungle he had just come from. But under closer examination, there was a difference. There were no blemishes. Everything was brand new, pristine. The colors were more intense and saturated. Every single leaf, every piece of bark was perfect and perfectly placed.

It was quiet, the same type of quiet one would experience during a winter snowfall where every sound is immediately absorbed by a thousand falling flakes. But the abundance of soft, green moss that carpeted most of the jungle floor and everything else for that matter was more likely the reason- even the animals remained quiet. It was cooler with no humidity, leaving the air fresh and clean like an ocean beach after a heavy rain. The most striking and pleasant difference was the lack of bugs. There were none as far as John could tell.

He raised his arm to brush his brow and was taken aback by what he saw. His arm's movement blurred slightly. He waved his arm around to reconfirm what he had just seen. Sure enough, his movements would blur ever so slightly, looking almost as if it were vibrating. He realized that he had seen this before but had no memory of it when he returned to the other side.

He took off in the direction he had taken in his first trip hoping to encounter once again some of the elders. He remembered that it was quite a distance, so he began to pick up the pace and jog. As he did, the trail ahead of him and the surrounding jungle blurred as well, not unlike moving about in street view on Google Earth. Time was certainly altered. He found he could travel great distances in a short amount of time with relative ease.

He noticed that there were patches of the trail where he could see through the jungle floor down to a mirror image of his surroundings. It was as if there were sections of the trail made of glass allowing him to peer down to the world below. It occurred to him that all those times in his life he felt as if he was being watched that perhaps he was. He stopped to study it and found the jungle below him was identical to the jungle around him. Just that the one below was rife with the normal flaws one would typically find in nature. He wondered if he was traveling through reality just on a different plane, a different level. He questioned which reality was the real, intended reality and was it possible he had been living in the wrong one all this time? At this point anything seemed possible, and nothing seemed impossible.

He reached the point where he had encountered the elders before. It was a place where the dense canopy broke open to the sky above allowing filtered sunlight to make its way all the way down to the jungle floor. Surrounded on three sides by a single giant, "U" shaped granite boulder some 100 feet long and 50 feet high. Near the top were three nautilus symbols carved into the it's cliff face. One nearly worn away and two others distinct and fresh. In the center of the back wall was a keyhole opening just large enough for a single, small man to fit through. Not unlike the many online games John had played, the lighting behind it was different, almost pulsating, drawing the player to what was the obvious, intended route. He looked around for the elders or any sign of life but there was no one to be found. Still there was an overwhelming sense that he was being directed to a yet unknown destination.

"Hello?" he called. "Hellooo?" he shouted a bit louder this time. Silence. He looked over towards the doorway. He would have loved to have had the advantage of some tangible guidance at this point, but he knew in his gut that once he entered that opening, he would be in uncharted territory and on his own. He also knew that once he got near enough to it to peer into the hole, that it would be a point of no return and he would be transported into whatever was waiting for him on the other side.

He could put it off no longer. He would have to go through that Alice in Wonderland rabbit hole if there was to be any hope of recovering his mom and Heylia. He approached it slowly and instinctually held his breath with each step forward fearing it could be his last. To his surprise he was close enough to touch the walls of the opening and still no change. He had to turn to the side and squeeze his way through. In a sudden moment of panic, he stepped back, back into the light of the court of the Elders. He gathered himself, breathed a sigh of relief and realized the doorway worked both ways. The realization that he could return the same way gave him a newfound confidence and he once again squeezed himself through, this time pushing himself all the way through.

He stood inside looking around with a hand still touching the doorway's edge. It was hotter, much hotter and damp. There was a pervasive smell in the air. John breathed in and made a face. It was not horrific, just not pleasant. He knew he had smelled that pungent smell before but was unable to place it. "Grandpa's old cigar ashtray!" he muttered, having suddenly remembered.

Most of the trees had been stripped of their leaves and many of them were charred from what he guessed were years of constant fires. The most significant difference was the lighting. It was muted and insufficient. The best way to describe it was that it had that cold, harsh, one lone bare bulb glare to it. Everywhere. It was as if the sun had been replaced with a single refrigerator bulb hanging from a frayed and gnarled wire. And there were bugs. Lots and lots of creepy, crawly bugs. It was the gray sameness of the landscape that made him realize finding his way in would be tricky and he needed to begin leaving some Hansel and Gretel breadcrumbs should he need to find his way back. He decided snapping a twig on each charred branch creating contrast of the black char against the inside exposed wood would be the easiest to spot on the way back. He set off ahead in a slightly downward direction snapping a twig every 20 steps or so. He looked up to see if he could determine the position of the sun for further direction but there was none. He noticed that where the sky should have been the other reality's jungle floor above him. He had entered a different plane that was now below reality instead of above it and he could physically feel it. There was a monotony of sameness, a lack of detail that added to the unexplainable pall while trekking forward. The heat, the humidity, the pressure... It was oppressive. He became aware that his exposure to that environment was beginning to affect his mood. John could feel himself slipping into an anxious, angry frame of mind and he began to consciously work against it. He knew he had to move quickly. He felt as if there was some sort of expiration date on his existence just by being there. He became more determined and more focused on what he had come to do. Find his mother, find Heylia and get out.

Not long into his hike he came across the first signs of life. It was not what he expected- houses or buildings of some kind but rather large, worn spots on the ground. He had come across a den where the Nephilim had slept. Scattered about were food scraps and crudely fashioned tools. He slipped behind a tree, held his breath, and listened. Whoever had been there had moved on and once again John cautiously continued down the trail. As he rounded the corner, he saw the first signs of an encampment. There was a fire pit with several crudely fashioned huts surrounding it. He could hear movement and once again slid behind a large rubber plant.

He looked beyond the encampment and noticed other groupings of huts scattered throughout the area. He could hear voices, but they were higher in register. It was the voices of women. Lots of women. There was no sign of Nephs anywhere.

"Where are the guards," he thought. After several minutes of observation, he decided to approach the hut that was closest to him. He hastily crept towards the back when he noticed that each step closer had become harder and harder. Each step required greater effort than the last. He stuck his arms out as if to test the air in front of him and it too required a greater than usual effort. It was like entering a pool. The deeper he got, the harder it was. Although he could see nothing, it began to feel as if he were swimming in molasses and to go any further might result in being completely stuck and unable to free himself. He backed up to where he was still able to maneuver and caught his first glimpse of life- a headful of auburn hair.

"Hey! he whispered. She didn't acknowledge him, so he called out a bit louder. "Hey!" Still no response. "Hey!! Nothing. "Pssssst!" Suddenly she turned. She looked right at him but still didn't see him. "Over here!" he shouted. She appeared to look in his direction but looked right through him.

In his frustration he over exaggerated his call. "PSSSSSSSSSST!!" She looked at him, her eyes grew wide in astonishment and an enormous smile spread across her face. He was able to freely walk towards her. He tried it again. "Pssst!" She ran towards him excitedly jabbering in Bislama. And then it dawned on him. The mysterious, mechanical hissing sound the villagers had made when he first entered the interior had a purpose. Its purpose was to clear a path allowing him access to the interior and now it was effectively clearing a path through this invisible, organic, semi-permeable boundary wall that surrounded their encampment. If the prison walls were so easily breached, why hadn't the women taken it upon themselves to escape? The answer would be found in the curious jars hanging from nearly every tree surrounding the perimeter. Filled with little white stones, the clear glass jars served as reminders to not even attempt an escape because the little white stones were not stones at all. They were teeth. Their teeth. It was standard operating procedure for new arrivals. As a precaution, the Nephs would remove most of the teeth of the women held captive. Its purpose was twofold. First, it denied the women of the only weapon available to them. It made the frequent forced mating less hazardous for the giants and secondly, it made it impossible for them to create the hissing sound that defeated the imprisoning barrier wall, making it virtually impossible for them to escape.

She was middle aged, a little lighter skinned than some of the other tribespeople with features more Anglo than most. To his dismay, as John drew closer, he realized her expression was less of happiness and more of crazy. Up close her eyes were wild. She was physically standing in front of him, but it grew apparent that mentally, she had long since checked out, retreating into her own safe and secure world of denial.

"Where are the others?" he asked. "I'm looking for a little girl and-" His sentence was cut short by a stifled scream coming somewhere in a lone bure nestled between two distant rubber trees. John immediately turned. First towards the sound and then back at his newfound friend. Her crazed, near toothless smile changed ever so briefly to that of fear but quickly returned to that vapid, distant gaze and overly exaggerated smile. She began to slowly walk away, retreating into the opposite direction of where the sound had come from. John looked back and began running towards this new distress signal.

He arrived to find the crude shack surrounded by a picket fence made of large bamboo stakes that had been sharpened at one end. The only other time he had seen something like it was on a prior trip with Aiden to New Guinea. The natives would construct a similar pen to trap and contain wild boar. Somehow John knew this was no wild boar pen, this was designed to keep humans from wandering off. As he got closer, he slowed at the sight of a large animal skin garment tossed to the side just outside the handmade door. Just around the corner were three young women sitting on a wooden bench. They were dirty, naked, and tied to one another. Their feet were bound to the legs of the large, wooden bench where they sat in silence. Their faces wore the look of fear and dread. Their deadened eyes that of resignation. John quickly scanned them to see if Heylia was among them. She wasn't. These girls were a fair amount older than her but perhaps they could shed some light on where she might be.

John stealthily made his way to the rear of the dilapidated shack and out of the girl's line of sight. He could hear the muffled sounds of someone or something inside the hut. He decided the best way to determine what was going on without setting off alarm bells was to climb one of the trees and peer down through the many holes in the run-down thatched roof. He found a loose picket in the fence, removed it, and quietly placed it on the ground. He began to slip through when he glanced back at the razor-sharp bamboo. "That would make one serious weapon should I need one," he thought. He reached back through the hole in the fence and carefully pulled it back through.

He made his way up the rubber plant and shimmied out a long branch that had grown directly over the top of the bure. He could see the top of the head of a half-naked Neph who was staring straight ahead towards the far wall. John slid out just far enough to get a glimpse of what had so intently garnered his rapt attention. Standing with her hands to her sides and head slightly down was little Heylia staring straight back at him. John was incensed and involuntarily gasped in horror. The Neph paused and then tilted his head as if listening for the sound to repeat. Instead, a new sound came, the sudden splintering of the very branch John was straddling. As if by reflex, John instinctively pointed the sharpened fence post downward to break his fall just as the creature looked up. With all his weight behind it, the pointed end entered his cow-sized eye and exited behind his left ear. John flopped on top of him still holding the post. He frantically jumped up trying to shield Heylia from the grisly scene. He held her head into his chest and quickly shuttled her towards the front door.

"Are you OK?" he asked. She nodded "Juthed Thcared," she lisped. John pulled back, gently cradled her chin tilting her head up. He smiled at her. "Everything's gonna be alright now. Do you know that where I come from there is a tooth fairy? And she comes and brings surprises for every tooth that's missing." She smiled as John wiped her tears with his shirt. "Go on outside and untie the other girls. We're gonna get you all home, OK?" As soon as Heylia turned from the doorway John, now standing over the Neph spat in his face. He was absolutely seething. In a final, parting gesture John placed his boot on his head and with all his weight, firmly seated the fence post into the dirty clay floor beneath him.

Using the markers of the broken branches as his guide, John led the girls back to the spot where he had entered. Heylia assured him she knew the rest of the way out and with that the girls turned and ran the rest of the way.

His mother was somewhere back there, and he was determined to find her. He quickly made his way back past that horrid shack where he had found Heylia and was taken aback at how quickly the flies had smothered the dead Neph's lifeless body. It had to be several inches in depth of flies covering his form from head to toe. He turned away from the gruesome scene and the disturbing sound created by a thousand feasting insects and followed the distant sound of rushing water. He rounded the corner of a group of oddly placed granite boulders that tumbled into a calm pool of river water. There, gathering water from the small, secluded eddy into clay pots was his mother. He looked about, scanning the bush for any signs of Nephilim but she seemed to be alone. John took no chances however and quietly made his way to a thick group of magnolia trees directly behind her.

"Pssssst!" he signaled. No reaction. He tried again but this time louder and with more persistence. "PSSSSSSSSST!"

"I can hear you," she said without so much as moving a muscle, "and if you do it any louder, they will hear you as well." She continued looking straight ahead and John could see her cheek rising from the side in a smile.

"Are you OK?" he said as he continued to scan his surroundings for Nephilim.

"They're planning something," she said. "Something big, I don't know what, but they seem more agitated than usual. They've been prepping for something...which is why they left me alone here." They're never too far away but they seem too busy to care of late."

"Well, that's great because we're getting out of here now, today," John said.

"Oh, I'm not so sure we could-" she was cut short by John,

"That's OK because I am. I am sure. We're leaving right now."

"It's just that it's been so long since I've been on the outside," she said.

"I know, it'll be scary, but others are waiting, Professor Wharton is waiting," John tried to reassure her.

"Wharton? Professor...Wharton?" she asked.

"Yeah, so far, he's the only one that knows I'm in here, he's the only one that knows where we'll exit. I told him I was coming to get you."

"Well, let's not keep him waiting," she said with a smile. She left her vases at the riverbank and quickly followed John into the dense jungle.

CHAPTER 18

HELLO AND GOODBYE

"Hello Miriam."

John and Miriam never expected *that* voice to greet them as they emerged from the bush. It was a voice with a French accent, it was familiar, it was the voice of Gerard, John's uncle. Standing on the beach, leaning on one of the many giant rocks that peppered that section of shoreline, an old Russian Mosin Nagant rifle slung over his shoulder. Miriam stopped; her smile replaced with the look of panic which was quickly replaced by the look of anger. John was confused. Professor Wharton was supposed to be there waiting. He was the only one who knew of John's plans to retrieve his mom. John was careful to hide his growing suspicions of his uncle.

"Hey, hi. Everything alright? Where's the professor? What are you doing here?" John asked.

"He's fine," his uncle flatly stated.

"If what you mean by fine is lying face down in the dirt unconscious..." a gravelly voice yelled from behind a boulder. It was hard to tell who it was. John thought it might be an injured Professor Wharton and started to run towards the voice, but he was mistaken. A bloodied and broken Fletcher Howard appeared from behind the rock and began to stumble over to where they stood. Gerard rolled his eyes.

"Must you?" he said, almost bored.

"Yes. Yes actually. I must and I will..." Fletcher said, pausing briefly to spit out blood. "Gerry."

"I'll handle this!" barked Gerard.

"Oh really? Like the way you handled everything at the trial?"

"Shut up!!"

"That didn't work out so well for me, did it? You said you had your boy here under control. You said he'd walk right in and we'd have 'em. Piece of cake."

"Gerard! How could you?!?" cried Miriam.

"Fils de pute!" chided Gerard.

Oh, shut up Miriam!" Fletcher's bloody face revealing a look of utter contempt. "If you had taken up with me rather than Frenchy here you could have had a normal life. A good life! But no, you chose him. *You* put yourself in that prison. You gave me no choice!!"

Gerard had heard enough. A lifetime of deceit was far too difficult to reflect upon and Fletcher's words were now becoming too much of a mirror. It wasn't going to get any prettier by allowing him to go on and he never much cared for Fletcher Howard anyway. He reached across his chest to the canvas strap that held the Nigant at his shoulder and was in the process of sliding it into position when Fletcher sprung at him like a hungry leopard. It caught Gerard by complete surprise and in an instant, Fletcher was somehow behind him and had ensnared his neck in the rifle's shoulder strap. One swift kick from the back to Gerard's groin and Gerard's knees quickly buckled and folded beneath him. Fletcher stomped his foot into Gerard's back and while still choking him attempted to turn the barrel towards John and his mother. John wasted no time and charged him. The crack of the round as it left the Nagant's long barrel made John instinctively throw his head to the left and as the bullet passed, it passed by so closely that he could feel the air being sucked out of his head. John was able to get behind him and apply a choking head lock he'd learned in one of his Aikido classes. He applied it just as he had been instructed and within seconds the struggling Fletcher Howard dropped like a 50lb bag of jasmine rice.

"It works. Holy shit, it works!" an out of breath John muttered. A recovered Gerard rushed the lifeless Fletcher intent on finishing him with his 5-inch survival knife, but Fletcher had one last hateful surprise in-store for his boss. A 7-inch knife of his own concealed in his boot now held at arm's length pointed directly at the charging Colonel. He jumped to his feet, extended his arm, and watched as Gerard ran himself onto the sharpened steel. There was a horrific look of disbelief on Gerard's face as the knife buried itself into his chest. Fletcher grabbed him by the collar and held him on the knife while staring at him. He tilted his head as if studying him. He had no doubt done this countless times in his mind and one got the sense that this long-awaited moment was a moment he was savoring.

John picked up the vintage rifle and slammed the heavy, wooden butt end into the eyes of Mr. Howard, sending him reeling backwards on his heels. His shoe caught the gnarled branch of a driftwood log that had washed onto the sand, sending him back onto a group of small boulders sticking out of the sand. The back of his head smashed against the rock with a sickening thud. John was convinced that there would be no more surprises. He turned back to his mom who was sitting in the sand and looked at her as if to say he was sorry. Sorry she had to re-enter the world she had left so many years ago only to witness such horror and disappointment.

"Are you OK?" he said gently.

She smiled at him and gently shook her head no.

"No. No, I'm not."

John looked down at her hands covering her stomach. They were bloody. Very bloody.

"No no no no no!!!

John scooped her up and began running towards the interior's exit point.

"It won't work that way. It's an exit." Miriam whispered.

"It has to work." an exasperated John declared. John lowered his head, exhaled, and stepped in. He laid her down on the soft, dry moss and began to tend to her wounds.

"I'm sorry. I'm sorry for everything" Miriam said through her tears.

"I can fix you."

I'm sure you believe you could," she said with a smile. "But I doubt it."

"I can!!"

I doubt it, John. *I...me. My* believing determines *my* fate. You cannot determine someone else's believing, no matter how well intentioned. You became such a handsome boy... Use your knowledge for good...for good..."

Her voice trailed off. She coughed; her breathing became elevated. She reached up and touched his face.

"Your father no longer needs to protect you. He'll join you soon and then I can finally rest. " She took a long, death rattling breath.

"I have my wish now."

Her eyes left his and quietly closed.

John felt a hand touch his shoulder. It was one of the three elders. "We shall tend to her. You must go now. They come tomorrow. You must stop them. There is a portal at the base of Mt. Yasur. They will come from there. They will come to do battle."

John wasn't hearing much of what they said. He was battling his own body that wanted to flood him with tears of despair and grief. The pressure behind the eyes, his nose beginning to fill, his throat clamped, desperate to hold himself in check. His brain trying to process the loss of his mom, the loss of the man who raised him, the outrage that accompanied the onset of betrayal as it replaced a lifetime of trust. It was all a bit too much to comprehend.

The second elder spoke.

"Come, we will show you a different way out."

"I can't. I mean not yet. I have to go back for Professor Wharton, he's hurt and-"

"We have attended to him. We will take you to him. Come. Hurry. This way."

In what can only be described as a conscious coma, John followed them without question and disappeared back once again into the interior.

CHAPTER 19

THE ARRIVAL

John found himself at the quiet place. He had discovered it when he first arrived and was finally well enough to wander about. It was on the outskirts of the village, elevated just enough to give an expansive overview of the peaceful valley floor. It was a rocky point where the foliage hadn't a chance to take hold. The rocks were too numerous, too smooth and moss covered but because of that, did provide some surprisingly comfortable seating where he would contemplate life and how it was turning out so far. He stood there looking out, his head lowered as he let out an involuntary sigh. It was impossible to do anything but consider the enormity of what lay before him. What was at stake for him, for Em, his friends- everyone. *Literally* everyone on the planet. What would a world dominated by these evil creatures be like? There was no way to even imagine it, but he knew that everything he held dear would certainly be ruined. It was no longer a choice of whether to do something or not. It was not an option to ignore it and go back to the way things were no matter how much he wished it so. There was no hiding anywhere. Anywhere. It struck him that he would give anything to go back, back to when his biggest worry was making the rent by the first or who was going to pony up for the next round at the Red Witch. He would have done anything to have this crushing weight taken from him.

He looked up. In moments of need even non-believers instinctively look up.

"I don't know how to pray," he said, shaking his head. "I never really learned. Sorry. But I could use some help here." He shifted his weight from one leg to the other and kicked a few pebbles off the edge.

"Apparently you have this law, believing, the law of believing. Apparently, I'm rather good at it. According to some people, *very* good at it. I don't get it; it just strikes me as common sense. It's always been a coping mechanism, just a tool for getting me through life. Nothing more. Surely there has to be somebody else that's as good- no, better! - than me that could do this job. Why do you need me, why do you need *my* toolbox?!

"I don't want to do this!" he yelled. "So, if there is any other way to...fix all this...well," he paused looking for the right words. "It'd be great if you could let me know... Uh, Amen."

"Amen," Em echoed, standing only ten feet behind. John smiled sheepishly.

"Well, how long have you been standing there while I was talking to myself like a crazy person?"

"You mean when you were praying- what any sane person would do in this situation. Get any answers?"

"Not a one."

"You know they're gonna turn tail and run at the first big Neph that shows his ugly face, right.?"

"The villagers? Yeah. Yeah, I do. But that's OK. I just need them to create a distraction, to give the Nephs the idea that there are thousands of warriors, just out of sight, waiting for them. We've got to keep them in that open field just long enough."

"Sister, huh?" Em asked.

"Shut up." John rolled his eyes. Em laughed that wonderful laugh that John found irresistible. John grabbed her by the sleeve, pulled her in and kissed her.

"I had very good reasons to believe that you know." He continued to hold her in tight against him. "I hope you have some appreciation for the amount of restraint exhibited in the presence of such extreme hotness."

"Thank you, compliment noted. Well, so many things make sense now." she said with a bit of relief in her voice. "I mean, you had me ready to enroll in self-esteem classes after that little... you know...at the Westin?" John feigned ignorance.

"The shower?" She punched his arm. "Oh my God! Are you blushing!?"

"Maybe. Can I take you on a date?" John asked. "I mean, *after* we save the world."

"Yes." she said. "Preferably dinner and drinks at the Westin." She winked at him.

There were a series of unnerving, minor tremors that took place on the day the elders had prophesied. The smiling faces of the villagers were nowhere to be found. Rumors had spread like wildfire and many of the women and elderly had already begun moving the children to the far side of the island. It was a precaution taken any time they sensed peril- like when a suspicious ship suddenly appeared on the horizon. It really wouldn't help if it all went south. There wasn't anywhere to hide from this. This wasn't a mystery ship on the horizon. It wasn't even an *armada* of threatening ships coming into view. There were no equitable comparisons, but it was a hip shot reaction and it kept the children preoccupied. The men spent time huddled in groups, sharpening their weapons, and painting each other with pigments just as they would before any large, seasonal hunt, their normal jubilance now replaced by hushed tones and fearful looks.

Then it rang out. From the leaping tower the sharp clang of metal on metal pierced the morning air. It was Kwanteef, high atop the tower sounding the alarm, the call to all warriors. It was a sound that they had waited for 70 years. It was the sound that should have announced the joyful return of the planes and their magical, wonderous cargo. Instead, it was the sound of impending fear, destruction, and doom. He continued banging the salvaged Willys wheel with a broken piece of its leaf spring as the men sprang into action. The ghost giants were coming, and they were coming exactly where the elders said they would. The villagers looked at each other wide-eyed in the realization that this was real, this was happening, and it was happening now. They scrambled to the edge of the clearing just inside the tree line and took up their predetermined positions. There was more than 300 of them, fiercely painted and poised in their most threatening stance. John looked about, satisfied that they were ready. Or at least as ready as they would ever be.

Gathered on the edge of the clearing John stepped forward to get a better view. There at the base of Mt. Yasur at the far edge of the clearing scattered between the piles of black and grey pumice were massive trees and brush but still no sign of the invaders. And then he saw it. In a camouflaged deer in the wood's moment, a 6 1/2-foot Neph appeared from out of the trees. Then another. And another, and another until there were more than 20 prehistoric looking figures standing with clenched fists. Then in unison, with the precision of a Rose Bowl parade marching band, they formed a large circle the size of two football fields. They stood motionless, now facing each other across the center of the circle. It was as if they were no longer concerned with the throngs of threatening warriors standing before them. Suddenly the sound of rushing wind filled the air. A swirling vortex of fog-like mist formed at the rocky base of the extinct volcano. The sun itself was partially blotted out and the entire landscape was bathed in that eerie light that comes during a lunar eclipse.

"Stanap stongfala!! Stand strong!!" John barked. He looked over towards Em standing with her hands at her sides, her feet slightly apart, staring straight ahead. If she was scared, she certainly put on a brave face. Such power, such grit he thought. She had more than one dog in this fight and her determination was front and center.

"God is she hot!" he thought. He immediately laughed out loud at the absolute absurdity of his thought process at a time like this. Em looked over at him, a slight question mark on her face which quickly melted into a loving smile. John crossed his arms across his own chest and pointed at her. She signed back. "Me too." The men took this as a signal of John's confident defiance in the face of danger and joined him, with a chorus of raucous, forced laughter, puzzling some of the Nephs.

Out of the swirling fog the silhouette of a man appeared. He was at least 14 feet tall and festooned with animal bones and skins. He carried a giant club at his side and slowly walked out of the haze, looking side to side at his soldiers surrounding him. He was truly an intimidating man, hideous looking- large garish, over-exaggerated features, his jet-black hair tangled and matted to his huge, bulbous head.

"Jesus!" John thought to himself, "this is right out of the book of Samuel, just like Ethan said."

John stepped forward and began walking towards him.

"What are you doing!?" Professor Wharton said through his teeth.

"They're not here for tea. They're here to kill us, to dominate us, to enslave us. I don't need to wait for him to spoon feed us that information. I'm going to introduce myself, so he knows who's spoiling his plan."

Suddenly the portal behind the beast closed. It closed with such force that the shock wave knocked everyone down. Everyone except Goliath. John quickly got himself back up and continued his walk towards the giant.

"No new players!" John said in a soft, sing-songy way like he did as a ten-year-old stickball player.

"Ok...now we know how many are on the team. No substitutes. Time to play ball," he muttered. As he made his way forward, he reached out and from behind a large rock grabbed a lacrosse stick that was leaning against it. He had fashioned it weeks ago out of a tree limb during his first recuperative visit. In fact, he'd made it from the same limb that Sam had stripped its branches from and gave him his lesson in believing and how for him, Kava was unnecessary. John had taken up lacrosse in school and he was about to find out if he was still any good at it. It would be the goal shot of a lifetime and he would either be carried out on the shoulders of his victorious teammates or in a coffin on his way to his own funeral.

He reached into his satchel and pulled out a perfectly round piece of volcanic rock. It was about the size of a softball and unlike pumice, was very heavy. It was the dense solid rock formed when Mt. Yasur spewed its ancient molten metal directly into the sea causing it to bead up into perfectly round balls. He placed it into the vine netting noting how much heavier it was than the small, unripened coconuts he had used to teach the villagers the game. The giant stood and watched him, mostly out of sheer curiosity. Why wasn't this puny human running away?

"Three-time Olympic gold medalist John Ferrum steps up for the shot... and the crowd goes wild!" he narrated to himself in his best announcer's voice.

He took a deep breath and exhaled as he spooled up the stick and its payload. Then with all his might, he released, sending the volcanic ball hurtling into the air. It was headed directly for the giant's forehead, a picture-perfect pass. Within seconds the projectile would lodge itself in his cranium, directly between his eyes, just above the bridge of his enormous nose and he would fall, dead before his gigantic body even hit the ground. That's the way it was supposed to be. It was the way John saw it unfold in his mind. Instead, the giant anticipated the trajectory and caught it a mere 12 inches from his face. He took the time to look at it and then, using both hands, he grimaced and popped it like a watermelon in a shop vice. It crumbled into pieces and they fell to the ground.

A large portion of the fearless warriors turned and high-tailed it back to the safety of the forest's edge. But Professor Wharton, Em and now Kwanteef and his party had stayed. Surprisingly, Sam slowly turned, his perpetual smile gone and slowly made his way back towards the airfield. John couldn't be mad at him for leaving. He was old and frankly, would probably just be somebody they'd end up having to rescue had he decided to stay and fight. There were now only a little more than twenty out of the three hundred warriors left.

"OK," John said with a sigh, "Plan B."

"What's the set up? -over." crackled the two-way. John pulled the radio from his belt, pressed the button, and responded, "Just like monkeys- perfect circle with King Kong dead center- over."

"ETA in 1 point 5- over."

"You know what to do Aiden."

"You should hear us now mate- comin' in hot!!"

The sound of a large prop plane drew all eyes skyward. It came directly over the top of Mt Yasur and immediately dove down the side of it, banking hard and to the left. When it reached the open field, it was nearly skimming the treetops.

Jay and Max were belted in but not in the way one would think. This was no comfortable passenger airliner with plush seats and overhead compartments. This plane was all business. And that business was hauling freight. It was a scuffed up, seatless aluminum shell with two powerful engines on its wings and nothing more. Without seats, the only belts they wore were safety belts that hooked them and their harness to a static line that ran down the entire length of the fuselage. They carved out a spot by the window and sat on one of the nearly thousand cases of powdered baby formula that had been spoiled in the excessive heat waiting for the various government agency approvals. What could have been an incredible life sustaining gift was now a problematic waste product looking for a willing landfill. Wasted because of bureaucrats and their miles of inane red tape. Not the first time and surely not the last but they were about to be put to good use. The guys would see to that.

"You know this stuff can be dangerous," Max shouted into his headset above the engine noise. "Have you ever seen that Cremora bomb video on YouTube?"

"Yes, I have," Aiden shouted back through the headset, finishing off mike, "and when this baby hits 88 miles an hour? Your gonna see some serious shit!"

Jay came on the com, "Hey is the glass in these windows distorted or somethin'?"

"No, why?" said Aiden.

"Cause these guys look...I dunno, bigger or somethin'. Like a lot bigger."

Ethan, seated in the co-pilot's seat raised his eyebrows and shot Aiden a knowing look. He unlatched his seatbelt and said,

"Time for me to head back and lend a hand."

"Be sure to hook up- don't want to drop you into that mess," Aiden smiled. He tapped the headset to broadcast to the guys in the cargo hold.

"Alright lads... showtime! Head to the back and open the hatch- you're gonna have to use the manual override. See that big red handle?"

"This is gonna be soooo funny!" Jay shouted at Max.

"We should be filming this!" he shouted back. Max reached into his back pocket and set his phone to video to document the beginning of their elaborate 'prank'.

"Do you see the red handle!" shouted Aiden.

"Yeah! Yes! we got it" Max shouted.

"Ok. Unfold it towards the back and then pull it straight down." Aiden instructed. The door abruptly flew open. Jay cautiously approached the edge and looked down over the drop zone.

"Holy shit! Dude they really are-"

"Go! Go! Go! Go! Drop! Drop!" Aiden shouted into the com. His bark was just the mind-clearing jolt the guys needed. They began to push pallet loads of the powdered formula out the door.

"Faster!!" Aiden shouted.

Aiden grabbed the controls and banked the plane into its tightest turning radius possible. At only 200 feet off the ground, every nut and bolt rattled and groaned in protest. Jay, Max, and Ethan fought inertia and struggled to unload the boxes. Max missed with one of the boxes and hit the support pillar to the door. It burst open and instantly covered all of them in the beige powder.

"Dude! You're missing them! Tighter! Tighter circle!" Jay screamed.

"Don't get your knickers in a wad Nancy! It's spot on, right where we want 'em" Aiden shouted. "Keep pushing 'em out! Faster!"

Aiden kept the plane in a tight, steep banked circle as the guys tossed out carton after carton. After several passes, the boxes were beginning to pile up, forming a sloppy haphazard cardboard wall behind the circle of warriors. The Nephs stood watching the plane with curiosity.

As everyone watched Aiden and his crew drop box after box with startling precision, John felt an overwhelming need to turn around. He gazed towards the tree line behind him. His eyes narrowed and he found himself staring at it for some reason, studying it. Suddenly, one by one the elders appeared, much in the same way the Neph's did. It was very much like one of those 'magic eye' pictures that required a concentrated stare while simultaneously defocusing the eye in order to see the hidden picture within the picture. Even as they approached, they seemed to be ever so slightly out of focus and John was unable to clearly see them as he saw others. Sam was back and it was as if he was leading them.

"Sam is an elder?" John thought to himself. The group of elders held back, hands clasped at their chests in an almost prayerful posture while Sam hobbled to the center of the palm frond floor covering the large pit Em and her fellow villagers had created. With his back to the remaining village warriors, Sam faced the large circle of Neph invaders, grasped the leather strap from which his nautilus medallion hung and ripped it from his neck. The very one he had forbidden John to touch while he was recuperating. Even with his crippled body there was an undeniable determination in his stance. He thrust his arm to the sky, the dangling medallion in his clenched fist and held it there. His thin, brown arm trembling- not in weakness, but rather defiance. He held it there, the glint of the sun catching the eyes of the enemy as it tossed and turned in the wind. He slowly placed the nautilus on the ground and turned to address his fellow villagers.

"It begins," he announced. "It begins with you, John Frum."

John, too tired to take Sam to task and correct him for the millionth time, stepped forward without comment.

"No John Frum!" Sam abruptly scolded. Confused, it shocked John, stopping him dead in his tracks. Sam looked him square in the eye, a sudden look of compassion coming over on his face.

"Your father."

And there it was. Professor Wharton, with tears in his eyes, looked to John and with an affirming nod, he silently took his place in the center. John stood in disbelief, staring at the ground trying to process this revelation. What happened, what had he just heard? He turned to look at Sam for some sort of explanation but looked just in time to see Sam's back as it retreated into the dense jungle. There was no time to think this through or to sort it out. He had to get back on task, back to the job at hand. His life, and the lives of others depended on it.

One by one the elders took their place in the circle, each standing behind one another until they formed a perfect nautilus shape. They placed their hands on the shoulders of the person in front of them signifying the solidarity, the union, the one in purpose of their mission. It was like hooking a number of psychic batteries together in series, John being the final contact point, the tip of the spear. From father to son the nautilus was finally complete, the believing of generations was spooling up for one final act.

John instinctively held his arm out pointing directly towards the gathering Nephalim. Suddenly his arm went out of focus. He realized that he was vibrating at an incredible rate. The boxes that were piled about the field began to vibrate as well. With each passing moment the vibration got more and more intense producing that weird, mechanical hissing sound. Suddenly they stopped. Suddenly all was dead silent. It was met with confused looks on the face of the Nephs.

Each elder closed their eyes and in the silence, although made by many, a singular sound of a solitary breath as it was being exhaled was the only sound to be heard. The first box broke the silence with a loud, startling pop. It shot a column of beige dust nearly fifty feet up into the air. Followed by another and another and another until like a mat of Chinese firecrackers it reached its peak culminating in a thunderous roar of continual explosions. Hundreds and hundreds of columns of the beige dust shot into the air until the entire bowl was filled with thick, choking baby formula dust. And then, once again, silence.

The Nephalim looked about and burst into uproarious laughter, brushing themselves off. That was it? That was the almighty Elders defense?

"Is that it? That all ya' got?" a voice rang out from the dust. In the thick haze a hobbling figure could be seen dragging himself towards the nautilus. It was a badly battered Fletcher Howard refusing to die, a beige ghost caught in some sort of cruel limbo. Cradled in his badly broken and bleeding arm was the bolt action rifle that had killed his mom. He was attempting to load it with his one good arm.

"You had your shot," he said, his speech slurred and almost unintelligible. "Last couple of thousand years... not too bad. It's their turn now... I have the key and there's nothing you can do about it!"

He raised his rifle up as high as his battered arm would go and squeezed the trigger. John could hear the thud as the bullet lodged itself in the bark of the gum tree directly beside him. It was unexplainable. Instinct would cause anyone else to take cover, but he didn't. There was no fear, not one iota of fear. He felt... Invincible.

"Kahore feaa! No Doubt!" yelled the professor as he glanced over at John.

"Anake whakapono! Only Believe!" John answered forcefully.

John was first to lower his head. He breathed in deeply and exhaled fully. Each member followed suit, each taking a deep breath and exhaling. The air surrounding the invaders seemed to take on a life of its own, ever building, ever increasing until it was the strength of a gale force wind. It was a Saharan sandstorm, only that of baby formula dust, the air chokingly thick with microscopically small particles. The once amused giants were no longer. Instead, they began to choke, dropping their weapons, covering their eyes and mouths with their hands desperate for some clear air. Any air.

Another shot rang out. Fletcher Howard had managed to squeeze off yet another round. This one almost found its target, actually grazing the outside of John's left ankle but his adrenaline infused body never felt it. He reached back into a basket that had been lined with pitch. In it was a torch made from a tree branch wrapped in a t-shirt soaked in, of all things, Kava and thick, black oil. The plan was to light the torch, throw it into the swirling dust storm and ignite the microparticles and anything standing in it. Every once in a while, the news would report on an unfortunate tragedy involving a grain elevator that hadn't been properly ventilated. Seems that when super-fine wheat dust reaches a certain critical dust-to-air ratio, a certain density, it creates optimal conditions for a very dangerous event. A spark would inadvertently be introduced by some poor unsuspecting sap and set off an incendiary chain reaction capable of taking out entire small towns. Others have documented this physical reaction on a much smaller, yet lethal scale using non-dairy coffee creamer agitated by a fan in a 55-gallon drum. When ignited, those micro-fine particles react like a cannon. YouTube is filled with idiots finding out the hard way just how big of an explosion it can produce. Knowing that does put a certain thrill into your morning coffee.

Well, that was the idea behind John's plan. Except he miscalculated one thing. To get the correct amount of solids to remain airborne, a great deal of wind needed to be generated. The same great deal of wind that was now preventing him from keeping his torch lit. Each time he would raise a burning torch and approach the dust storm it failed to stay lit. At his third attempt and subsequent failure, he raised his head in frustration. It was then he saw an object in the sky. It made no sound but was in the shape of a small airplane. It quickly came into view, flying directly over the elder's nautilus formation and was making a beeline towards the ever-growing dust bowl.

"Oh my God, it's Sam!" Em shouted.

It was Sam, about 200 feet up and draped in his sacred Sponge Bob-Square Pants robe. Around his neck were the coveted neon, glow-in-the-dark rave necklaces the villagers were so fond of, on each of his fingers, glistening ruby-red ring pops adorned each knuckle. And what self-respecting royal would venture out without the finishing touch of a hot pink, 'We're # 1' foam finger crown perched atop his head?

"He's flying...a plane... that doesn't fly," a befuddled Em exclaimed "It's a prop! A bamboo prop. That's... impossible!"

"Pretty sure *he* doesn't think so," Professor Wharton remarked.

Slung around Sam's neck was his goatskin satchel that housed many of the vintage artifacts he'd picked up over the years, many from the servicemen and women that had abruptly left so long ago. One such article was Sam's magical fire box. It was an old brass colored Zippo lighter. On one side the remarkably preserved red and black circle logo of Lucky Strike was still visible, on the other, a raised relief of Rita Hayworth in a polka dot two piece, her top almost completely worn off. He removed it from the bag, opened it and with his thumb, struck the wheel against the flint. One would probably think that after seventy years the chance of the lighter fluid still being fluid and that it would still be combustible were pretty slim. Considering Sam was *actually* flying a large-scale model airplane constructed entirely out of bamboo and jungle vines through the air tells you that Sam's operation of the immutable law of believing was firing on all cylinders and old lighter fluid was not going to be given even the slightest consideration. The spark lit the wick and its classic blue and orange tipped flame persisted even in the face of buffeting wind shears thanks to its patented stainless steel windscreen. His plan was to approach the giant dust storm from above, drop the lighter down into the swirling haze and quickly turn back, making his escape to safety. Up to that point all went according to plan. Except as he dropped his flaming magic fire box, the wind caught it and threw it back up and over his head. Sam quickly looked about but it was nowhere to be found. He felt a sudden burning on his wrist. Then on his knee. It was the hot, burning pink ooze coming from above his head, dripping down on him. The lighter had become lodged in one of the folds of his royal headdress and flames had already engulfed the raised finger portion of it. As the fire grew larger, flaming pieces of pink foam blew back and onto the tail section, igniting the 70-year-old bamboo like Carolina fatwood.

He looked back at the ever-increasing fire and quickly realized there was little he could do now. But Sam too had a plan B. He looked down over the unbroken nautilus, his birds eye view allowing him to really see the significance of its shape. Starting from the center, a seed and working its way outward, getting stronger with each ever-expanding, overlapping wall until it's end. He reflected on how he had carried that nautilus pendant as long as he could remember, hoping that one day it would be complete. That day was now here. He had led a good life and had lived to see the return of his Messiah. How could anyone ask for more?

He banked the bamboo plane to the left and entered into a steep dive. He began chanting loudly "USA, USA, USA..." and disappeared into the swirling mass.

John and the villagers stood in horror as Sam's flaming plane dove into the thick dust. The moment he disappeared; every sound was sucked out of the air producing a deafening silence you could actually feel. John, suddenly realizing what was about to happen, turned to Em and yelled, "Now Em, NOW!!"

In one fluid motion Em reached behind her head, drew her machete from its canvas sheath and sent it hurtling towards the thick rope vine wrapped around the large gum tree. Like watching lightning inside a distant thunderhead, a small orange flash was all the warning they would get as the machete found its target, severing the vine in one clean swoop. The entire palm frond floor beneath the nautilus suddenly let go, dumping everyone unceremoniously into the large pit she and her fellow workers had dug. A tremendous roar and bright yellow wall of flame raced across it's opening. The heat was so intense that much of everyone's hair had been singed and whatever scant clothing they wore gave off small wisps of pre-combustion smoke. The blast produced such a sonic boom that most everyone was rendered partially deaf. That was a gift however, as it served to block out the horrific screams of the few remaining Nephalim who were not fortunate enough to die instantly in the blast. John was the first to recover and scrambled over to Em to make sure she was all right. He reached out to her, cradling her head in his arms. She began to cry but then quickly got herself back in check.

"We have to check on the others," she said softly.

"Funny place to take a nap!" a voice bellowed from above. It was Aiden surrounded by the guys. "Come on, let's get you out of this hole. Little Em... you alright, luv?" He lowered a makeshift ladder and John helped each of the Elders out. Professor Wharton took his turn and paused to look at John. John wordlessly motioned for him to head up and then helped Em, following directly behind her.

It was a horrific sight even with the thick smoke obscuring most of the gory details. Lying before them was a scorched, barren wasteland, much of it still on fire. Bodies and pieces of bodies were everywhere. But the worst was the smell. The smell of burning human-or more accurately- almost human- flesh was something that could never be forgotten. It so permeated the air that one could taste it in the back of the throat. They stood in silent disbelief at the degree of devastation. As far as the eye could see there was nothing left. As the winds began to shift and move the curtains of smoke, the first glimpses of Sam's smoldering wrecked plane became visible. It was nose first in the ground and had pinned what remained of Fletcher Howard's charred body, still holding his stolen rifle.

In a sudden realization Em sighed, "Oh Sam." The sadness was overwhelming. Professor Wharton, echoing Em's sentiment,

"Sam." Aiden reached out and put his arm on the professor's shoulder. He quickly shook it off prompting a look of surprise from the group. "No! Sam!" he said emphatically and pointed into the thick cloud of grey smoke. Just barely visible was the silhouette of a short, slight man making his way towards them. It was Sam- his foam finger crown reduced to a pink blob of hardened goo in his hair, his Sponge Bob Square Pants sacred robe looking anything but. He raised both arms victoriously and shouted,

"Whakapono!"

That's my bloody robe!" Aiden protested.

"Yeah," John said. "But he doesn't know that." John looked at Aiden, a bit of confusion on his face. "Long story."

Sam stood before the group, a huge smile on his face.

"YouTube? I be on YouTube?" He immediately launched into his spirited version of "God Bless America" accompanying himself with a display of his dancing prowess. It was a sight to behold.

CHAPTER 20

JUST WHEN YOU THOUGHT
IT WAS SAFE

B ack in the village everyone was packing to go. John limped over
to where Ethan, Max and Jay were sharing a single, precious
beer.

"Ferrum, we save the human race from alien monsters and all
you've got is light beer?" whined Max. Jay shook his head.

"After what we've been through this is about the best beer I've ever
had! So how long have you known about...all this? What's th-" John
cut him off.

"It's a long, long story. Certainly, one that needs more than one
beer to tell."

"Sorry about your dad dude, er, uncle. We just heard," said Ethan,
"but how does somebody turn like that? Helping the very people that
want to exterminate you? It doesn't make sense, there's no excuse on
God's green earth for that."

John thought for a moment. "You're right. There is no excuse but there's always a reason. And for an especially long time I'm gonna have to try and figure that out. I think that some people just want to matter. They want to be important so badly that they'll do just about anything."

"Ok, but why you? Why are they after you?" asked Max.

"Because he's the only one that can stop them," interrupted Aiden as he walked by. "The only one that can prevent them from carrying out their plan. Do you know why he's the only one? Hmm?" He paused for dramatic effect. "Because he's the only one who doesn't know he can't." Aiden's eyes narrowed, his head nodding, reading each of them to see if his profundity had landed correctly. It hadn't.

"Well, anyway I promised you boys I'd show you the wonders of Koontal firsthand. What better way to do that than partaking of a bit of Kava with the rest of the village? Went to visit Miss Edna and wouldn't ya' know she provided all the right stuff God rest her soul," he crossed himself and shot a knowing look at John. "My own special brew- they're mixing it up as we speak."

Professor Wharton and John's eyes met. Professor Wharton began to move towards John but was abruptly stopped by John's upheld hand.

"Don't." he mouthed and turned his back towards him.

"You're John's father," Em stated rather matter of factly.

Professor Wharton smiled sheepishly, nodding his head affirmatively.

"All this time..." Em continued. "I'm sorry, I never knew, you never said-"

"I... had to protect him...from them. All the while hiding from them myself." He paused, carefully choosing his words. It was a story that he hadn't been able to tell for such a long, long time. "Charles Wharton disappeared one night in the jungle. No one knew why. He was my friend. I searched all night. I walked out of the jungle the next morning exhausted and some very bad men called me by his name... held me by my throat, wanting to know where John Ferrum was. They spent years...searching...for me. Hell, I even helped them search. As soon as I could, I left to go back and look after John. Been doing that ever since...in the only way I knew how. The only way I *could* and still keep him safe. Do you know how hard it's been just watching him, not being able to reach out and... now, this..."

"We'll both eventually find our way into his heart." Em said.

"I have a sneaking suspicion you've already beaten me to it. Put a good word in for me, will you?"

Em coyly smiled, leaned in, and whispered, "Not sure I'll need to." She looked over his shoulder.

John had been standing behind them, listening. The professor turned and smiled. John was the first to offer, his arms opened. He and his dad embraced; the professors' eyes closed.

"You're staying?" John asked. The professor paused and nodded.

"Yeah. Kinda' belong here. They need me and..." an even longer pause, "Maybe I need them more."

"That doesn't leave me much of a choice now does it?" said John. "I mean...you'll probably need some help."

They both stood grinning at each other. Aiden sauntered over.

"Before we raise a pint in victory you might want to have a look-see at this." Aiden reached inside his flight jacket and produced an old, torn parchment. There were symbols in faded ink written across it that weren't readily identifiable.

"Where'd you get this?" asked the professor.

"Paid a visit to Fletcher Howard's campsite on the way here. Didn't think he'd mind if I borrowed a few things. And if my Miss Em is as smart as she says she is..."

Em shot him a look and grabbed the leathery parchment from him. She walked to the window to get more sunlight on it. She studied it in silence then turned back to them. Her face grimaced.

"What?" Aiden queried.

"Theoretically this was supposed to have come out of the satchel we snagged in DC at the Smith, right?" she asked. "But we only got half of it. So, this is..."

"The very one. It's the missing half, right?"

"It is."

"That's good, right? What does it say?"

She stood there just looking at the ground as if searching for the words.

"Em?" Professor Wharton tried to encourage her out of her trance.

"Buckle up." she said, still staring at the ground.

"Buckle up? That's what the document says, buckle up?" John asked. "What does that even mean?"

Em took a deep breath and sighed.

"All... that?" she said pointing in the direction of the decimated field they just came from. "That was the hors d'oeuvres, the trailer to the movie, it was the-"

"Wait! All that?! All that was-"

"The rehearsal. A dress rehearsal for the big show, the main event."